THE CASTLE OF BERRY POMEROY

By Edward Montague

The Citizen: A Hudibrastic Poem (1805)
The Castle of Berry Pomeroy (1806)*
The Demon of Sicily (1807)*
Legends of a Nunnery (1807)
Modern Characters (1808)

* Available from Valancourt Books

THE CASTLE OF BERRY POMEROY

𝔄 𝔑𝔬𝔳𝔢𝔩

BY

EDWARD MONTAGUE

Nought is there under Heaven's wide hollowness,
That moves more dear compassion of the mind,
Than beauty brought t'unworthy wretchedness,
By Envy's snares, or Fortune's freaks unkind.

SPENSER.

TWO VOLUMES IN ONE

VALANCOURT BOOKS

The Castle of Berry Pomeroy by Edward Montague
First published London: William Lane, 1806
First Valancourt Books edition 2007
First paperback edition 2014

Published by Valancourt Books, Richmond, Virginia
Publisher & Editor: JAMES D. JENKINS
http://www.valancourtbooks.com

The Library of Congress has catalogued the hardcover edition as follows:

Montague, Edward, fl. 1806-1808.
 The castle of Berry Pomeroy : a novel / by Edward Montague. – 1st Valancourt
Books ed.
    p. cm. – (Gothic classics)
 ISBN 0-9792332-5-9 (*trade cloth*)
 I. Title.
 PR5029.M787C37 2007
 823'.7–dc22

                              2007002740

ISBN 978-1-941147-13-9 (*trade paperback*)
Also available as an electronic book.

Cover: An anonymous sketch (after Thomas Girtin, 1775-1802) in ink,
graphite, chalk, and watercolor, of Berry Pomeroy Castle, Devon.

Set in Adobe Caslon 11/14.3

INTRODUCTORY NOTE

The Castle of Berry Pomeroy was first published in 1806 in two volumes at William Lane's Minerva Press. Its title page attributes the novel to "Edward Montague, author of Montoni, or the Confessions of the Monk of St. Benedict, &c."

This attribution is problematic, as *Montoni; or, The Confessions of the Monk of St. Benedict* did not appear in print until two years later, in 1808, and its title page declares it the work of one "Edward Mortimer."

The cross-attribution of *Montoni*'s authorship, together with the similarity of the two names invites speculation that Montague and Mortimer were one and the same, and although there is no proof of it, both names have the ring of pseudonyms, both being drawn from the annals of English history.

Montague is credited as the author of *The Citizen: A Hudibrastic Poem, in Five Cantos* (London: J.F. Hughes, 1806), *The Legends of a Nunnery: A Romance* (4 vols., London: J.F. Hughes, 1807), *The Demon of Sicily: A Romance* (4 vols., London: J.F. Hughes, 1807), and *Modern Characters: A Novel* (3 vols., London: G. Hughes, 1808). In addition, if we tentatively credit him with Mortimer's two works, we can add to this list *The Friar Hildargo: A Legendary Tale* (5 vols., London: J.F. Hughes, 1807) and *Montoni* (4 vols., London: J.F. Hughes, 1808).

The idea of a single man penning so many volumes in the span of two years is difficult to accept and invites speculation that the same pseudonym might have been used by more than one writer, or that some of the works may have been collaborative in nature. It is worth noting that nearly all Montague's works were published by James Fletcher Hughes, whose authors very often wrote pseudonymously. For example, Hughes regulars included "Mrs. Edgeworth", "Mary Anne Radcliffe", and

"Caroline Burney", attempting to profit from the successes of Maria Edgeworth, Ann Radcliffe, and Frances Burney. Hughes, who was renowned for his unscrupulousness, would hardly have balked at affixing the names of Edward Montague and Edward Mortimer to a book, regardless of the work's actual authorship.

And yet, although Montague's identity and the details of his life remain shrouded entirely in obscurity, his works have occasionally been dusted off and issued in new editions. The infamous publisher of pornography, William Dugdale, released a double-column reprint of *The Demon of Sicily* in an undated edition (circa 1841), complete with lurid and explicit illustrations. And *The Castle of Berry Pomeroy* was resurrected in a "Second Edition" in 1892. This curious edition was printed at Totnes, at the Times and Western Guardian Offices, by "T. & A. Mortimer." I have been able to locate only two copies of this rare edition, one at the University of Texas, and one in my own collection.

The present volume follows the first edition of 1806, specifically, the copy in the Corvey Collection. The only two copies of the first edition I have located are those at the Corvey and the British Library.

The text is reprinted here verbatim from the first edition, except that a few minor typographical errors have been silently corrected. No effort has been made to modernize or standardize punctuation, spelling, or grammar. Other errors, such as the mysterious change in De Clifford's name from Thomas to Henry, have also been retained to maintain the flavour of the original text, which bears signs of having been written hastily.

Finally, I should note that this edition was a collaborative effort. I would like to thank Ryan Cagle for typing the text of the novel and Joseph Jarvis for proofreading it.

James D. Jenkins
Chicago
March 31, 2007

THE

CASTLE

OF

BERRY POMEROY.

𝔄 𝔑𝔬𝔟𝔢𝔩.

IN TWO VOLUMES.

BY

EDWARD MONTAGUE,

AUTHOR OF

MONTONI, OR THE CONFESSIONS OF THE MONK OF ST.
BENEDICT, &c.

Nought is there under Heaven's wide hollowness,
That moves more dear compassion of the mind,
Than beauty brought t'unworthy wretchedness,
By Envy's snares, or Fortune's freaks unkind.

SPENSER.

VOL. I.

LONDON:
PRINTED AT THE
Minerva-Press,
FOR LANE, NEWMAN, AND CO.
LEADENHALL-STREET,
1806.

THE

CASTLE OF BERRY POMEROY

CHAPTER I.

"Often are the steps of the dead in the dark eddying of
blasts, when the moon, a dull shield from the east, is rolled
along the sky."

OSSIAN.

IN the west of England are yet to be seen the ruins of Berry
Pomeroy Castle, formerly a place of great strength, but now,
like the proud ancient possessors, almost forgotten, and daily
mingling with the dust.

Many are the dark deeds said to have been perpetrated within
its walls, as the yet blood-stained stones and flitting shades that
nightly hover over their sad remains, entombed amongst the
ruins, or buried without sepulchral rites, are sad mementos of.
Often do their wailing shrieks vex the nocturnal breeze, that
else would sleep in the quiet amidst the shady branches of the
surrounding woods.

But more horrible than all, dwell on the affrighted air the
dreadful groans of the blood-stained Sir Ethelred de Fortebrand,
cut off by the just decree of an avenging Power, in the prime of
his years, by the keen dart of the assassin.

Soon as the vapours of the night condense upon the earth,
appears his melancholy form wandering amidst the ruins, under
whose cumbrous weight, in the silent vaults beneath the chapel,
are his murdered remains.

Close by his side, condemned for ever to wander on the earth, restless and miserable, stalks the shade of the guilty Lady Elinor de Fortebrand: and when the gale brings on its broad pinions the hollow sounds of the distant Abbey clock of Ford, when it tolls for midnight prayer, then do the furies arise, armed with writhing serpents, whose death-darting tongues glisten with poisonous venom, and whose pestiferous breath instantly blasts each herb and flower: with these they lash with horrible yells the shrieking shade of the Lady Elinor, and then lay her beside the murdered Sir Ethelred, on sharp quick-piercing brambles. Thus is her guilty spirit condemned to endless tortures, the due punishment for her horrible deeds. Silent, solitary, and restless, glides among the hanging woods, the pale, ghastly form of the Abbot Bertrand, the cruel and deadly instrument of the Lady Elinor de Fortebrand, cut off, when he least expected it, by a most horrible death, the just reward of his atrocious actions.

Such are the reports which the neighbouring peasantry have handed down to their offspring, and who, to this day, relate to the traveller the sad tales.

The Castle is beautifully situated on a rising ground, its western turrets overlooking the neighbouring wood, and the spacious plains of Dartmoor; to the south is seen afar off, the waves of the great Atlantic ocean, bringing on its agitated bosom the rich treasures of east and western climes.

The northern and eastern towers hang over a luxuriant vale, the sides of whose steep boundaries are cloathed with hanging oaks and aspiring beech trees; at the bottom is seen a transparent sheet of water, which loses itself amongst the thick crouding trees, on whose green summits the well-pleased eye reposes with delight, till the sweet windings of the romantic Dart seduces the attention of the enamoured beholder. The bountiful hand of nature has adorned this spot with all that can please the sight, and animate the mind to the adoration of Him under whose masterly direction the creation rose.

Strange and horrible it is to tell, that this place, so fitted to calm contending passions, and convey a soothing serenity to the mind, should have been the spot where foul murder, hatred and envy, deceit, and every base passion of the mind, instigated by the fell demons of darkness, held their dread abode.

In this Castle, beloved and respected by all who knew him, and the favourite of his sovereign, long lived the noble Sir Hugh de Pomeroy. His Lady dying, left him a widower, with two daughters, Matilda and Elinor. With parental care and tenderness did the venerable Sir Hugh procure such preceptors for them as those dark ages afforded. Father Oswald, who had for half a century resided in the Castle, assisted by his instructive voice, the sage councils of Sir Hugh. Their persuasive precepts sunk deep into the heart of the beautiful Matilda, who, at the time this history commences, had attained her eighteenth year.

The Lady Matilda was of a middling stature, elegantly formed; her mild blue eyes, sweet dimpling cheeks, the abode of the blushing rose; her coral lips, that when opened, displayed their ivory inmates, and her auburn hair, falling in curls over her polished forehead, and confined behind in glossy tresses by strings of pearl, captivated each sighing heart: but while she innocently spread the tender inquietude around, her own heart was free as the midway air. She had yet to learn what it was to love other than her dear father and sister; she was the possessor of every virtue that ever adorned the female breast. To the poor tenantry she was a benevolent and generous assistant; and out of the stipend she received from Sir Hugh, supported many an aged peasant, who lifted up each hour their trembling hands to heaven, calling down its blessings on her head.

But different was the figure and disposition of the Lady Elinor; she was of an unusual tall stature, her beautiful dark brown ringlets overshaded her high forehead; and her animated dark eyes, her acquiline nose, and majestic form, commanded respect. She was one year younger than the Lady Matilda de Pomeroy, and was of an overbearing disposition; her rage, whenever contradicted in her pursuits, violent in the extreme; her passions oft bore her far from female delicacy in their resistless sway.

Elinor's commanding beauties gained her more admirers than the retiring soft charms of the Lady Matilda; but many, when they perceived how much she was the slave of her ungovernable passions, ceased in the ardour of their protestations.

The Lady Elinor, under the specious mask of friendship, bore the most deadly hatred against her sister, whose only crime was that of being the heiress to her father, Sir Hugh's, extensive domain.

The feeble lamp of Sir Hugh's life had long borne an uncertain light; the vital powers that still animated it seemed nearly exhausted; and at length, convinced that he was now summoned to render up his life to Him who gave it, he called his daughters to the side of his couch, and having given them every advice for their future conduct in life, and prayed heaven to bless them, he closed his eyes in the silent sleep of death.

Words would fail in their weak attempts to describe the agonizing heart-breaking grief which shook the tender frame of the Lady Matilda de Pomeroy, and had nigh hurled reason from her seat; but the divine Providence, who heaps not on us more than we can bear, gave to the lenient hand of Time the power to calm the dreadful agitations occasioned by the loss of her beloved parent.

Not so the Lady Elinor; a few tears were all she dropped to the memory of her father; and she viewed with impatience, not grief, the illness of her sister, because it prevented his will being made known.

At length, when the sorrows of Matilda had subsided into a silent melancholy, and she was thought able to bear it, the will of Sir Hugh was perused by Father Oswald, in the presence of her household.

But what was the rage and disappointment of Elinor, to find that she was left entirely dependant on her eldest sister, to whom descended, in lineal succession, the estates and domain attached to the Castle of Berry Pomeroy!

Her passion knew no bounds; openly she taxed the Lady

Matilda with having, by her arts, so seduced the affections of her misguided father, as to cause him thus to neglect her.

The Lady Matilda vainly endeavoured to stem the impetuous torrent of her anger; she advanced to Elinor, and throwing her arms about her neck, said—"Oh, my beloved sister, think you our sainted parent conceived that what was bestowed on one was not equally so on the other? Yes, dearest Elinor, Matilda can enjoy no happiness without your partaking of it."

Elinor scornfully turned aside from the warm embrace of her sorrowing sister.—"'Tis right for you," said she, "to attempt to extract the barbed arrow yourself have planted; but I am fated to endure the rankling torture of the wound; and to be looked on by all around as the unportioned, neglected Elinor."

The Lady Matilda, finding all her remonstrances of no avail to restore peace to the agitated bosom of her sister, retired to her chamber.

CHAPTER II.

"With rustling sound
A monstrous boar rush'd forth; his baleful eyes
Shot glaring fire; and his stiff-pointed bristles
Rose high upon his back. At me he made,
Whetting his tusks, and churning hideous foam.
Then, then Hyppolitus flew in to aid me;
Collecting all himself, and rising to the blow,
Pierc'd his tough hide.
The monster fell, and gnashing, with huge tusks
Plow'd up the crimson earth."

SMITH.

SEVERAL months now passed, and at length the Lady Matilda once more began to revisit the world. Frequently would she stroll unaccompanied through the beautiful woods, admiring the wonderful works of Providence, as she viewed the sun sinking behind the western hills, or watched his glowing rays as they gilded the summit of some lofty hill.

Absorbed in meditation, she one evening exceeded her usual walk, and found herself deeply involved in the mazes of the forest. Much alarmed by this circumstance, she endeavoured to retrace her way back, when rushing full upon her, to her fear-struck eyes appeared a wild boar, who in an instant threw her to the ground.

The senses of Matilda had fled, and she was on the point of being tore to pieces, when, swift as lightning, rushed from an adjoining thicket a man, who, with his spear, transfixed the savage monster, and laid him breathless on the earth.

Quick as thought, he conveyed Matilda to a neighbouring spring, where, bathing her temples with the cool wave, he soon restored her to animation.

A deep blush suffused her cheeks on finding herself in the arms of a stranger; and quietly rising up, she, in animated terms, thanked her generous preserver, whose intelligent countenance beamed with delight at the protection he had afforded her: he now offered her his arm to support her, and which Matilda, weak and faint with the great agitation she had experienced, was obliged to accept.

"To whom, gallant stranger," said she, in a faint trembling voice, caused by the dreadful agitation she had undergone, "am I indebted for this wonderful preservation?"

"My name, Lady," said he, viewing her with looks of admiration, "is Sir Thomas de Clifford; and happy do I esteem myself that the events of this evening have afforded me the supreme happiness of rendering a service to the Lady Matilda de Pomeroy, whom, I believe, I have now the honour of seeing."

Matilda had often heard of that noble family; and now it occurred to her, that the possessor of the estate which bore that name, and which was but a few leagues distant from her Castle, had lately arrived to it; and from the noble appearance and deportment of the stranger, she was well assured that it was to him she was indebted for her life. She had once slightly cast her eyes on his face, and felt interested by the assemblage of manly graces which adorned it.

She blushed as she met his ardent gaze, and greatly confused, cast her eyes on the ground. De Clifford perceived her agitation; and though the sight of her beauties fascinated his admiring eyes, yet he instantly, though with difficulty, debarred himself the indulgence.

Thus reserved, they reached the Castle of Berry Pomeroy, when De Clifford, having entreated permission to wait on her the next morning, gracefully took his leave, and retired to his Castle by the winding path that led through the vale below.

The Lady Matilda saw him pursuing his way down the romantic steep; soon did the intervening trees hide him from her view. A deep sigh escaped her breast, and she felt unhappy, though she was ignorant of the cause.

She retired immediately to her chamber, and being fatigued with her long walk and the affright she had undergone, endeavoured to seek repose in the arms of sleep. But again did the occurrences of the day rise to her imagination, again did she see the horrid boar, with foaming tusks ready to devour her, and again did she behold the interesting countenance of De Clifford, and once more did a sigh escape her bosom at his ideal departure.

These delusions lasted till the sun, penetrating the casement of her chamber, awoke her with his gladdening beams. Hastily arising from her couch, she prepared to dress. Her auburn tresses were soon confined in braids, which encircled her head, and her beautiful forehead was lightly shaded by waving ringlets; she seemed to take more care this morning in adorning her lovely person than was her usual custom; the reason as yet she knew not herself.

Hardly had she concluded her morning repast, when she beheld De Clifford approach the Castle, by the same path he traced, after he had taken his leave of her the preceding evening. The mantling blood rose to her cheeks, as from the casement she viewed his interesting form. The dark plume he wore waved with the gentle breeze, and shaded his animated countenance.

Sir Thomas de Clifford soon entered the western hall, whither the Lady Matilda, informed of his arrival, met him. At first, a degree of constraint prevailed, and the conversation turned on the usual topics; but the polished ease and deportment of De Clifford's manners soon made Matilda lose her embarrassment, and she conversed with him with that ease that marks the well-informed mind.

If De Clifford was before captivated with the uncommon beauties of the lovely Matilda, the attraction was greatly increased by the accomplishments of her mind: and almost before he knew it himself, he had surrendered his heart as a tribute to her charms. At length, having greatly protracted his visit beyond the common bounds, he took his leave of the Lady Matilda, and they parted mutually regretting the loss of each other's society.

The enamoured De Clifford seldom passed a day in which he did not visit the Lady Matilda, who at length found an intruder in her bosom, who had taken too deep root to be extirpated. She would watch with delight the moment she saw him winding through the valley; and then, as if by accident, would direct her steps that way. Frequently they used, attended by the Lady Matilda's domestics, to stroll into the deep recesses of the wood; and unalloyed by a thought of the future, they passed the happy moments in admiring the romantic views around, or in observations on the greatness and goodness of Providence.

In one of these excursions, De Clifford, turning into a narrow path, took the hand of the surprised Matilda, and having imprinted an ardent kiss on it, fell on his knees before her.— "Will the Lady Matilda excuse this abrupt disclosure of a passion lasting as my existence, and pure as the heart I long to possess? Adored Matilda! yes, from the first moment I beheld thee, I loved! and my ardent love for you increases each moment I exist! Deign, oh angelic maid! to lend a pitying ear to my protestations of love and adoration, which will only cease with my existence! Tell me, at least, adored Matilda, that you do not despise me."

"Rise, De Clifford," said the Lady Matilda, her lovely countenance suffused with crimson blushes at the avowal of his sentiments. "The memory of my dear departed parent is too fresh, too green in my recollection, to allow me to listen to such a converse: be assured, I shall ever be most grateful to you for having preserved my life from inevitable destruction."

De Clifford, perceiving from the speech of the Lady Matilda, and her blushing confusion, that there were hopes his ardent passion would not be unregarded, and feeling the delicacy of her situation, after having imprinted an ardent kiss on the trembling hand he held, said—"Beautiful Matilda, suffer me to hope that I may one day have the celestial happiness of calling you mine; and although it may be distant, yet the bright prospect will cheer the tedious hours that intervene, and give me new existence."

In the intelligent countenance of Matilda, De Clifford saw with delight no traces of disapprobation, or discouragement to his suit; and respectfully returning her fair hand with a lightened heart, rose up, and the domestics appearing, they pursued their walk.

CHAPTER III.

"Glorious hypocrisy! what fools are they
Who, fraught with lustful or ambitious views,
Wear not thy specious mask."

FRANCIS.

"Dissimulation dwells,
As at her home, in every smile he wears."

SEWELL.

"Jealousy and love,
————————Thou eldest of all passions,
Or rather, all in one, I here invoke thee:
Where'er thou'rt thron'd, in air, earth, or hell,
Bring me to my revenge, to blood, and ruin."

DRYDEN.

RETURN we now to the Lady Elinor de Pomeroy, who, after she had heard the will of Sir Hugh, her father, read, proceeded to her apartments, with a heart overcharged with malice, and desire of revenge, against the Lady Matilda. In the rage of her distempered passion, she uttered some threats of a dark and dreadful import against her innocent sister, whose only crime was that of being first born.

But this was the cause that had stirred up the baneful passion of envy in her heart, and had broken the ties of sisterly affection in her breast.

The Lady Matilda stood between her and the means of the gratification of her avarice and ambition; and ill did she brook to see the voluntary adoration and respect which the numerous vassals paid to their beloved lady; and so degenerate was her mind, that no entreaties could prevail on her to forgive the slightest mark of disrespect in the retainers and peasantry, but would punish them with the utmost severity.

The Lady Matilda, to whom this injurious treatment was represented, fearful of increasing the dreadful passions of her sister, would make the unhappy sufferers every reparation for their wrongs, without disclosing to Elinor even her knowledge of her transactions.

Elinor now seldom quitted her apartments, but brooded in her restless mind on dark revenge, and the means of securing to herself the envied possession of the domains of the Castle of Berry Pomeroy.

Amongst the brotherhood of Ford Abbey was one Father Bertrand, who, for his seeming sanctity of manners, and voluntary penances, was surnamed the Pious. He would sometimes attend with Father Oswald, to assist in the performance of mass in the Castle chapel, and when in his religious exercises, seemed to be exalted beyond the earthly sphere. But the quick piercing eye of Elinor saw imprinted on the countenance of this Monk, in legible characters, dissimulation, and was assured in her own mind, that his religious deportment was only pretended, that he might, when the present superior died, be initiated in his situation, the gift of which was invested in the possessors of the Castle of Berry Pomeroy, as the lands and the abbey itself belonged to its domain, and was given to the Monks, by an ancestor of Sir Hugh de Pomeroy, for a residence, at a trifling charge, supposed to be as an atonement for some crimes he had committed.

The Lady Elinor now resolved to dismiss the venerable Father Oswald from the office of her confessor, and to have Father Bertrand as her spiritual director.

The Monk, with joy, obeyed her summons, and Elinor was soon convinced that she had rightly surmised with respect to his character and views; and she now saw that she had got a fit tool to assist her in whatever plans of villany she might wish to undertake.

Father Bertrand, who saw, in his acquiescence to the desires of the Lady Elinor, a certain prospect of advancement to the situation he had so long and so earnestly desired, hesitated not to unfold his diabolical designs towards the Lady Matilda; to which Elinor, whose mind was hardened to all acts of villany, if by them she could obtain her ambitious wishes, denied not her assent, and which a new circumstance, that we shall relate, urged her to hasten the completion of.

From the domestics who attended her person, she learned the frequent visits of Sir Thomas de Clifford to her sister the Lady Matilda; and wishing to see and know his purport in his daily attendance, she contrived to be, as if by accident, in the hall when he came.

It so happened, that the meeting took place the next morning after De Clifford had confessed his passion for her lovely sister.

His countenance, animated with delight, as he, approaching the Lady Matilda, made his respectful obeisance, and the blushing confusion which was visible in her countenance, soon convinced Elinor of the situation of their hearts.

With evident emotion she viewed the interesting and elegant form of De Clifford. The assemblage of manly beauties he possessed, forcibly interested her regards, and in his fascinating conversation she felt a secret delight and interest, such as she had not felt before.

When De Clifford had departed, and she had retired to her apartment, his elegant form still seemed before her—still did his animated converse sound in her ears; so powerful were his attractions, that they made even the proud heart of Elinor confess their sway. Sighing, she felt she loved—loved to adora-tion, the man who, with agonizing sensations, she perceived her hated sister would soon be the happy possessor of. Horror-struck at the idea, she exclaimed—"Rather may the yawning grave instantly swallow me up in its merciless jaws, and bear me to endless tortures, than bring that day to my view, which gives De Clifford to the envied Matilda!"

Father Bertrand now entered her apartment; he gazed on her agitated countenance with astonishment; he saw that something new and unusual had occurred; and assuming the most respectful solicitude, he enquired the cause.

For some time Elinor was silent; rage, grief, and despair, had denied her the power of communicating the feelings of her tortured breast even to this her friend in iniquity.

"Father," said she at length, "words cannot express what I suffer. Oh, De Clifford! shall I, must I, impotently resign the extatic thought of calling you mine? Shall I let Matilda, the hated Matilda, possess all that can charm the enraptured senses?—Oh no, no, forbid it, fate! Now, Father, assist me—prevent the union—bring De Clifford at my feet—erase from life's busy page Matilda, and become the envied superior of the Abbey of Ford!"

The wily Bertrand saw with joy his ambitious designs beginning to mature; he wished the Lady Elinor to possess the domains of Berry Pomeroy, and his fertile imagination instantly devised a scheme which would at once effect that purpose, and secure to himself the elevated station of Abbot, without being in fear of the changeable disposition of the Lady Elinor.

With the hardihood of experienced villany, he now proposed to the Lady Elinor de Pomeroy to administer, at some convenient opportunity, to the unsuspecting Matilda, a composition of a deadly nature, which would chase away the vital spark of animation in such a manner as not to leave a suspicion of the foul means which had effected it—"And then," continued he, "though for a season grief may disturb the bosom of Sir Thomas, yet the superior charms of the Lady Elinor will soon erase from his mind the departed Matilda; and you, lady, will be the happy possessor of these lofty towers, and the amiable De Clifford."

Though for a moment a sensation of horror, at the dreadful means to be employed to effect her purposes, glanced over the heart of Elinor, yet her ambition and love for De Clifford soon made her deaf to the feelings of pity; and she consented to the diabolical project of depriving a sister, who tenderly loved her, of existence.

Thus does the dark fiend steal on the yielding heart by slow degrees, and which at length he entwines with chains of adamant, making it subservient to his fell purposes.

CHAPTER IV.

"Had I but died an hour before this chance,
I had liv'd a blessed time; for from this instant
There's nothing serious in mortality.
All is but toys. Renown and grace is dead.
The wine of life is drawn, and the mere lees
Is left this vault to brag of."

SHAKESPEARE.

"Oh, she is gone! the talking soul is mute!
She's hush'd! No voice, no music now is heard.
The bow'r of beauty is more still than death—
The roses fade; and the melodious bird
That wak'd their sweets, has left them now for ever.

LEE.

DE CLIFFORD, by his tender assiduities, brought from the Lady Matilda a confession of a reciprocal passion; and at length the happy day was fixed which was to make him the adoring possessor of her fascinating charms.

De Clifford passed the intervening time in anticipating the happiness the possession of the loved object of his soul would convey to him: smiling prospects of years of delight arose to his enamoured view; his whole soul was wrapped up in the delicious expectancy of hours of halcyon joy and bliss; and he seemed to swim in a sparkling sea of tumultuous raptures.

Matilda, whose heart so well approved her consent to unite her destiny with De Clifford, viewed the engagements she was on the point of entering into with a trembling agitation; the sacred purity of that solemn ordination impressed her mind with religious awe; and, with a beating heart, she perceived the day fast approaching, when, at the altar, she was to become his for ever.

But short-lived, broken ere mature, are sublunary joys! When we think we hold the phantom Happiness in our grasp, it recedes from our touch, and vanishes.

Such was the fate of De Clifford: with unutterable joy did he on the day preceding that appointed for his union with his adored Matilda, direct the necessary preparations to be made. His numerous vassals and retainers, by whom he was greatly beloved, shared in his happiness; all was gaiety and mirth at his Castle: and now the shades of night began to envelop the earth in its murky darkness, when a breathless messenger from the Lady Matilda informed him that she was dying, and wished to take her last adieu of him, while her fleeting spirits yet allowed her the power.

As when the moon, while with its bright beams it gladdens the face of the creation, and spreads its beauties over the silent world, is suddenly covered by a black cloud, which eclipses its silver light, and spreads a horrid gloom around, making night hideous—so fell the countenance of De Clifford, when, with frantic exclamations of soul-afflicting misery, he rushed out, and mounting his fleetest courser, which was soon covered with foam, arrived, with deep distraction imprinted in his features, at the Castle of Berry Pomeroy.

Wildly he rushed into the hall; no one there met his view; the place seemed deserted. Hastily traversing it, he ascended the grand staircase; and at length a confused sound of melancholy moans met his ear. He knew too well the cause of them; they smote to his heart an icy chill, and ran over his frame; and with difficulty he staggered on in their direction, and entered the chamber of the Lady Matilda de Pomeroy, where she lay oppressed with the cold hand of Death, surrounded by her weeping domestics, in the arms of Lady Elinor, having just received extreme unction from the hands of Father Oswald.

De Clifford flung himself on his knees at the bedside; he

grasped her hand, on which he imprinted a thousand kisses; and then, in the wild delirium of grief, smote his burning forehead in the excess of his agony, while he exclaimed—"And is this, my Matilda, our promised joys? Spare, oh gracious Powers, spare my adored angel! Can you look on, and not rescue her from the jaws of death? Speak, oh speak to me, my affianced wife! Behold thy wretched De Clifford! Oh Matilda, my lovely, my adored wife, live to bless me, or let me die with thee!"

Here his emotions became too great for utterance, and with a tearless eye, he gazed on the almost lifeless form of Matilda, while his whole frame was convulsed with his internal agonies.

Matilda, struggling with the chilling hand of death, fixed her eyes on him: for a long time the heart-rending tortures of such a meeting rendered her incapable of speech; at length, finding her moments limited, she thus, though with great difficulty, her powers being nearly exhausted, addressed him—

"De Clifford, do not give way to unavailing grief; spare me, in this awful moment, the additional pang of witnessing them! Live, De Clifford, live to make happy with thy worth some more fortunate woman! That happiness is denied me—even now I feel the awful hand of death! De Clifford, may the divine Author of my being, into whose hands I soon shall resign my soul, bless thee as I do—may he——"

Here, oppressed with excruciating agony, Matilda paused; for some time she remained motionless; at length, returning signs of life were perceived. She again fixed her eyes on De Clifford, and seemed to attempt to speak; she moved her lips, but no utterance came forth; her respirations grew shorter and shorter every convulsive heave; and at last, faintly pressing De Clifford's hand, with a deep sigh the breath of life escaped her.

The affectionate domestics, who had long suppressed their grief, fearful of disturbing the last moments of their beloved mistress, now with distracted shrieks bewailed her loss. Elinor had fallen into a fit of such long continuance, as at length excited general alarm; and she was conveyed, apparently lifeless, to her chamber, where she lay for many hours in a state of insensibility.

In the extremity of grief, De Clifford long gazed at the inanimate form of her whom he so tenderly adored. No tear, no sigh escaped him; his soul-harrowing fate, in thus losing, at such a moment too, the beloved idol of his heart, left not a vacuum in his mind unfilled by unutterable anguish; the measure of his woes was now full; silently he kissed the cold corpse, turned up his eyes to heaven in fixed despair, and with a deep and hollow groan, sunk lifeless by the side of his worshipped Matilda.

Father Oswald now directed the domestics to take away from the chamber of death the lifeless form of the wretched De Clifford. Silently they conveyed him into an adjoining room, where, laying him on a couch, they proceeded to use means to restore him to life: for a long time their efforts were in vain.

At length a deep-drawn sigh announced that life still lingered in his veins. Suddenly he opened his eyes.

"Oh God, where am I?" said he. "Who are ye that surround me? Even now I was with my adored wife! Wretches, ye have taken her away from me, but at the furthest verge of the earth will I seek her!"

He now sprang furiously from the couch, but was prevented from entering the chamber of the departed Matilda by the servants. Long time did he attempt to resist their endeavours to restrain his arms, and prevent him from doing some violence to himself. At length, wearied out with his exertions, and his internal agony, he sunk insensible on the floor.

When he again shewed signs of returning animation, Father Oswald, who had performed the last duties to the deceased, attended by the side of his couch, to endeavour to comfort him, and compose the dreadful agitations of his mind.

De Clifford, opening his eyes, fixed them for awhile on the Father, and seemed as if endeavouring to recall some circumstances to his mind. At last he exclaimed, in a low, hollow tone—"And is she gone—gone for ever? Tell me truly, Father, is it so? or is what I have seen but a horrible delusion?"

"The will of God be done!" piously returned Father Oswald. "The Lady Matilda sleeps in peace, and it is sinful in us weak mortals to repine at his Almighty will!"

"Oh, my Matilda, no more will your loved voice gladden my delighted ear—no more will my eyes dwell with delight on your charms!—Gone, all gone!—claimed by the cold grave! That voice, that dwelt in honied accents on my ravished senses, no more will speak comfort to the forlorn, deserted De Clifford! Oh, miserable wretch that I am—condemned to unutterable woe, and black, unceasing despair!"

Nature, at last wore out, relieved the miserable sufferer by a flood of tears. Father Oswald rightly conjectured that the unhappy De Clifford would be relieved by this vent to his grief, and silently beheld the big drops of anguish as they coursed down his pale cheek; and as soon as he judged it proper, had him borne in a litter to his Castle, whither he attended him himself.

CHAPTER V.

"Such is the fate of guilt, to make slaves tools,
And then to make them masters, by our secrets."

HAVARD.

" 'Tis only when with inbred horror
Smote at some base act, or done, or to be done,
That the reviling soul, with conscious dread,
Shrinks back into herself."

MASON.

FATHER BERTRAND, who saw his ambitious wishes near their completion, delayed not to prepare a potion such as would best answer his purposes in removing the Lady Matilda; for that being done, he felt himself secure of the situation he so much desired, as the Lady Elinor would then be able, from the power vested in her as heiress of the domain, to appoint him to the situation of Abbot of Ford Abbey.

He saw too, that being privy to the murderous transaction, he would have the Lady Elinor completely in his power; for he well knew the reputed sanctity of his manners would effectually screen him from the eye of suspicion.

Elinor, who saw, or thought she saw, the speedy fulfilment of her views, with regard to becoming the possessor of the domain of Berry Pomeroy, and also of being the happy wife of De Clifford, a strong inducement, which the wily Monk had advanced as a certain event, felt no sensations of horror when she received the fatal phial from Bertrand, and only waited for a moment, when, without exciting suspicion, she could administer it to her unsuspecting sister. The beloved image of De Clifford, ever before her eyes, was an inducement which spurred her on to the accomplishment of the dark deed.

Guilt is ever fearful;—from the moment she had determined on terminating the existence of her innocent sister, she imagined every one who saw her could read the dreadful purposes of her heart; and for a long time, in her chamber, she shrunk from observation.

At length, when she found the day was fixed that would, should it arrive, annihilate both her fond hopes, of possessing the estate and De Clifford, who would then, in addition to the horrible reflection of being the husband of her sister, be Lord also of the domain, she formed the desperate resolution of putting her foul intents into execution, but could not find an opportunity to effect her purpose without detection, till the day before that appointed for the nuptials; she then contrived, while at dinner, to convey the potent liquor into her sister's beverage, which she saw, with demoniac satisfaction, the unsuspecting victim drain to the bottom.

The powerful mixture soon began to shew its dreadful effects; and in less than an hour after she had taken it, Matilda was carried to her bed, from whence she never rose.

Hardened as was the heart of Elinor to the dark crime, yet she could not hear the dreadful groans occasioned by the excruciating pains the mixture produced, without, now that it was too late, regretting the foul deed.

But when she saw her sister almost in the cold arms of Death, fervently imploring heaven to shower down its blessings upon her, her fortitude entirely forsook her, her ambitious views faded before her, she forgot the beloved form of De Clifford, and in the height of her distraction, tore her hair, and dashed herself on the floor. Several times was she on the point of disclosing her crime to her expiring sister, and entreating her forgiveness; but the cautious Bertrand, who saw the internal agitation of her mind, and dreaded lest she should unfold the fatal secret, cautioned her, in a low whisper, to beware how she conducted herself, lest she should make known what would consign her to the powerful arm of justice.

Self-preservation made her hearken to him; and though it was difficult, in that moment of horror, for her to conceal the part she had acted in that melancholy scene, yet did she suppress the secret that swelled in her breast for utterance.

But when she, at length, saw she held in her arms the life-less form of her murdered sister, whose pure spirit from above now hovered over her guilty head, overcome with sensations of indescribable horror, she became nearly as inanimate as the pale form before her.

Bertrand almost repented the part he had taken; for though he had no fears of being amenable to justice for the horrid trans-action, for he well knew he could clear himself, yet he foresaw that the bare suspicion that would light on him, would sully that fame he had acquired for his religious observances, and become an insurmountable bar to his ambitious views.

As soon as he saw she had fallen insensible by the side of the bed, he immediately directed the domestics to convey her to her chamber, fearful that on her reanimation, some words of regret for the foul deed she had perpetrated, might escape her wandering senses.

Cautious and vigilant in the extreme, he, on pretence of

their presence being necessary in the last sad offices due to the deceased Matilda, removed all the domestics but one, a simple damsel, whom he knew was too ignorant to be an object of fear.

For a long while he feared that all his deep-drawn schemes would be rendered abortive by the death of the Lady Elinor, for as yet she shewed not the smallest signs of life, and scarcely was the faint pulsation in her arm perceptible.

He now applied some powerful remedies for her recovery, for he had made the medicinal properties of herbs his particular study; and at last, by their potent effects, he succeeded in restoring her to animation.

At length the Lady Elinor opened her eyes, but the first object they perceived being the Monk, she closed them again with horror.

"Foul demon of darkness," said she, "avoid my sight! Hearest thou not the dying groans—seest thou not the quivering pangs of Matilda? But for thee I should be innocent—now it is too late— already do the furies seize on my forfeit soul!—Ha, take back the phial, I will not give it.—What, has she drank it all? Where is De Clifford? See, she blesses me—me, who—oh horror! horror! horror——!"

Here, with a violent shriek, she again fell back, senseless. The affrighted attendant was hastily leaving the apartment to summon more assistance, but was forbid to do so by the Monk, who saw now that all his bright hopes were on the point of being for ever annihilated, and all his long-expected honours pass from his view, like the uncertain visions of the night.

He again, though with much difficulty, restored her to animation, and was pleased to see that her senses had not forsook her, which, he feared, from the distracted sentences she had uttered, was the case. She now breathed only deep-drawn sighs, which too evidently shewed the intense sorrows of her heart.

The wily Monk was too nice an observer of human nature, not to know that the first burst of sorrow and repentance being over, the mind of Elinor, possessed of what she had so long sighed for, namely, the unlimited possession of the domain and estates of her sister, would soon forget the rugged path she had travelled over to arrive at the summit of her wishes; he therefore left her to the unrestrained indulgence of her grief and lamentation; and he waited with impatience till the first excess of her sorrow and contrition for her foul deeds being over, he could soothe the anguish of her heart, by recapitulating the enjoyments she would now possess as the fruit of them.

When, therefore, having watched the opportunity, he breathed the name of De Clifford in her ear, and the hope there now was of the consummation of her wishes, the long-cherished idea, as if by magic, began to restore tranquillity to her mind; and while his fascinating manly beauties rose to her imagination, the regret she had for her atrocious act gradually diminished, and the pleasing attainment of her ambitious views soothed the storm that raged in her breast.

Bertrand now mentioned to her the great necessity there was for an immediate interment of the departed Matilda, as all fears of a discovery of her untimely end would be done away.

The Lady Elinor acquiesced in the propriety of this step, and early the next morning the sad remains were deposited, with great solemnity, by a train of monks, who attended from Ford Abbey, in the sepulchral monument of her ancestors.

CHAPTER VI.

"————————All days
Henceforth are equal;
To-morrow, and the next, and each that follows,
Will undistinguish'd roll, and but prolong
One hated line of more extended woe."

CONGREVE.

"Of comfort let no man speak:
Let's talk of graves, and worms, and epitaphs,
Make dust our paper, and with rainy eyes,
Write sorrow in the bosom of the earth."

SHAKESPEARE.

"There is a joy in grief, when peace dwells in the heart of the sad."

OSSIAN.

THE senses of the unhappy De Clifford seemed, for a long time, to endure a total stagnation; the soul-afflicting certainty that his angelic Matilda was lost to him for ever, reduced him to the deepest abyss of misery, from which not even the kind attentions of the venerable Father Oswald could recall him.

For a long time he refused all nourishment; his manly form began to grow weak and languid; his eyes, that used to beam with expression, were now sunk inanimate in his head; his countenance was haggard, impressed with deep furrows of despair; and his sorrowing domestics feared that their beloved Lord would soon follow his adored Matilda.

Father Oswald, who feared his senses would fall a victim to his long-continued grief, sought to tranquillize his agitated mind by the mighty precepts of religion.

"We must bow," said he, "submissively to the all-wise decrees of the divine Disposer of events, and curb the excess of our afflictions, when it pleases his supreme wisdom to deprive us of what

constitutes our happiness in this transitory world. To murmur
at his will is sinful: learn, oh De Clifford, to bear with fortitude
his decrees; resign thyself to his Almighty direction, who, only,
knows what is best for us. Shall we, short-sighted mortals, who
can scarce claim the present moment as our own, shall we, by
guilty repining at his ordinances, bring down the anger of Him
to whom we owe our present existence, and who created us to
obey and serve him?"

De Clifford would listen to the consoling converse of Father
Oswald, and though he owned the justness of his remarks, yet
did he feel a secret wish for a speedy dissolution of his corporeal
frame, that he might ascend into the bright realms of celestial
bliss, and there unite his kindred soul with his angelic Matilda's.
Life was now an oppressive load to him, who had no connexion
on earth to make him desire to remain on it.

But, at length, the persuasive arguments of Oswald, to a mind
sensible of the duty it owed to its Creator, began gradually to
have the desired effect on the heart of De Clifford; and, at the
expiration of two months, he began to feel a returning serenity
in his mind, which lulled the more poignant and distracting
emotions of his grief into a melancholy calm. He could converse
with Father Oswald on the subject so near his heart, without
relapsing into those dreadful deliriums of grief and despair
which, till now, had always been the result of such discourse.

As soon as he was able to leave his chamber, the attentive
Father would lead him out into the romantic glades which
surrounded the Castle, and there endeavour to draw his mind
from the continual contemplation of his misery, by pointing out
to him the beauties of the surrounding scenes, which presented
themselves to the pleased sight.

Sometimes ascending a rocky eminence, they would behold
the sweet windings of the Dart, which, in some places, was
diminished to a narrow stream, meandering through the arches
of the trees which hung on its bank; and, in others, swelling
in broad sheets of water, whose trembling bosom reflected the

radiant beams of the sun with tenfold brightness. Afar off would they descry the distant vessels gliding over the immense expanse of the Atlantic, till the intervening waves hid their tall masts from the strained sight.

The numerous cottages, the abode of peace and contentment, that lined the banks of the gentle Tyn, the peasants busied in ensnaring the finny tribe that sported in its clear waves, and the lofty spires of Ford Abbey, rising out of the green bosom of the thick surrounding forest, afforded a prospect which conveyed a peaceful calm to the agitated mind of De Clifford, who would, for a moment, forget, while contemplating the varied beauties of nature, the sorrows of his heart.

In one of these rambles, having ascended a lofty hill, De Clifford, turning his eyes towards the well-known spot, discovered the lofty towers of Berry Pomeroy Castle.—"O God!" exclaimed he, while bitter tears coursed down his pale cheeks, "behold the tomb of all my hopes! Alas! beneath those walls lies the cold form of my sainted Matilda, whom these aching eyes must never more behold!"

With forlorn and desolated feelings he stood for some time viewing the Castle, which brought to his mind the hours of delight and happiness he had passed there, never more to return; and thousands of tender remembrances of her, whose loved form for ever dwelt in his heart, and served to remind him of the total destruction of all his happiness, rushed to his too faithful memory.

He now turned, with a melancholy deep seated in his wan face, on Father Oswald—"Father," said he, "I owe much to you—the tribute of a grateful heart receive—but grant me one more kind service—conduct me to the tomb of my Matilda, that, on the spot that contains her sacred dust, I may give vent to my grief—deny me not this comfort, which I feel will ease my breaking heart."

Father Oswald for a long time combated this melancholy desire of De Clifford; for he perceived, as he spoke, an indescribable wildness in his eyes, which made him fear that he meditated some horrid act.

"For what purpose," said he, "would you again wish to rouse the sorrows of your heart, that, happily, in some degree have subsided? Ask not of me what in prudence I cannot, dare not consent to—your present agitation shocks me—what is it you meditate? Oh, De Clifford, is it thus you have disregarded my advice?—Reflect well before you seek to enter on such a rash undertaking—reflect what you might be guilty of, in the wild paroxysms of your distempered grief."

"Father," said De Clifford, "if you knew how much my heart is set on paying this last tribute to the beloved memory of my Matilda, you would not refuse my request. Believe me, you shall have no cause to repent your acquiescence;—I feel when that sad duty is over my mind will be more composed."

De Clifford accompanied these words with such a look of earnest entreaty to the Father, that, at length, he promised to comply with his desires, to endeavour to procure the key of the burial vaults, and attend him to those melancholy abodes.

De Clifford pressed the hand of Father Oswald with gratitude for this indulgence, the idea of which he dwelt on with pleasure, as though he expected to behold the animated form of her whom, alas! he had seen claimed by the powerful arm of Death.

Father Oswald saw, with great surprise, the encreasing contentment that appeared in the expressive countenance of De Clifford, and, at times, he would greatly regret that he had offered to procure him the means of visiting the tomb of Matilda; he, therefore, delayed that period as long as was possible; and when, at last, he was obliged to consent to the encreasing importunities of De Clifford, he procured the key, and appointed the next night to attend him to the abodes of death.

Towards the close of the day, De Clifford descended into the spacious hall, which he slowly paced, waiting with anxious expectation for the long wished-for opportunity of breathing his door of his dungeon opening, he was summoned to appear before the Baron. He followed in silence the person who commanded the party, and, retracing his former steps, arrived in the hall.

Here, in a chair of state, surrounded by the officers of his household, sat the Baron of Manstow. When he saw Walter enter, he looked at him with an enquiring eye, and then, in a stern voice, demanded what he had to alledge in defence of his too evident crime, in the murder or detention of Fitz-Morris?

Walter, at this demand, awoke from his seeming lethargy, and, endeavouring to collect his spirits, firmly replied—"My Lord, I am, as yet, ignorant of the purport of your words—journeying from London to the sea-coast, I was seized near your domain, and forcibly detained in your castle; and am now accused of a circumstance of which I have not the least knowledge.—I pray you, my Lord, that it may please you to unfold your meaning to me, that I may frame my replies accordingly."

"Not the least knowledge!" returned the Baron, in a voice of thunder—"vile slave, do not thy clothes condemn thee? confess thy crime this moment, or tortures shall wring it from thee!"

Walter now, in an instant, saw the dangerous and alarming predicament he was in. He immediately concluded, that the murdered body he had seen in the chamber, when he was making his escape from the bloody purposes of Roland and Ruffo, must have been that of the above-named Fitz-Morris; and the clothes which he had found there, and had put on, it was plain had belonged to him, since they had been the cause of his being taken, and suspected of his murder.

He would instantly have unfolded the whole affair, but he was fearful, that, in the search at the house, the jewels of the Fitz-Auburne family would be discovered, which Roland and Ruffo had taken from him; and that they, if taken, on examination, would, most probably, confess how they had been obtained, which would immediately discover him to the eye of justice; since he could not hope to be released on his bare word, but would, without doubt, be detained till the whole affair was elucidated.

Thus situated, he determined not to unfold the circumstance, but again declared his ignorance and innocence of the whole affair.

"How then," said the Baron, "did you obtain those clothes, which Fitz-Morris wore when he left this castle?"

"I purchased them," said Walter, "of a pedlar, my own being wore out."

"Villain!" exclaimed the Baron, "this paltry evasion is of no avail; declare, this moment, the whole of the bloody deed, or dread my vengeance!"

"I do, again, solemnly declare my innocence of the charge alledged against me," returned Walter.

"Put him to the question then," said the Baron.

Walter turned pale at this order; but, recollecting that his life depended on not divulging the circumstances which had come to his knowledge, he determined to persist in his ignorance.

Four men now laid him on his back, on the stone floor of the hall, and held down his hands and feet; a large weight was then placed on his breast, and the Baron, after a while, demanded if he would confess his crime?

Walter struggling with the difficulty of respiration, replied, he could not confess a crime of which he was innocent.

"Increase the weight," said the enraged Baron; "we will find a way to punish his obstinacy."

Another weight was then added, which, forcing the blood to the extremities, poured out in a torrent from his mouth, his nostrils, and his ears. After he had remained in this situation some time, the Baron again demanded if he would divulge what he knew of the transaction in question?

Walter, turning his blood-shot eyes on the Baron, after a long pause, which proceeded from the agonies he endured, again, in a faint voice, declared his ignorance of the charge.

"By heavens, caitiff, but you shall confess your crimes!" said the Baron; "and, as you seem so reckless of my vengeance, your tortures shall be yet still more encreased."

A third weight was now put on him; and, no longer able to endure the misery, Walter was struggling for utterance to declare he would disclose what he knew of the transaction, when the Baron, seeing the convulsed state of his body, and fearing that he was expiring, gave orders to his domestics to take the weights off, and to bear the prisoner back to his dungeon.

The moment Walter heard the Baron give orders to stop the punishment, he was inwardly pleased that he had not declared his knowledge of the circumstances relative to the murder of Fitz-Morris, which another minute's endurance of the dreadful agony he suffered must have forced him to do.

Not being able to move when the weights were taken off his body, the domestics helped him up; and, some restoratives being given to him, he began to recover from his pains. The Baron now exhorted him to confess, without further tortures being applied to his body, as, on the day after the morrow, he would again be brought before him.

Glad to hear of the delay, which he hoped might afford him some means of escape, Walter still persisted in his ignorance of the affair.

The haughty Baron, motioning to the domestics to bear him away, withdrew from the hall; and Walter was carried to his dungeon, where, some straw being thrown on the floor, he was laid upon it, with a pitcher of water and some bread by his side.

The harsh gratings of the key now turned in the rusty wards of the lock, and the bolts, as they were forced into their holds, echoed dismally, while the receding heavy tread of the men who had borne him to the dungeon, sounded along the vaulted passage. Soon all was quiet, except the solitary pace of the centinel, who guarded the door without.

Walter, now left to his own meditations, saw little chance of his being able to conceal the circumstances he was acquainted with, relative to Fitz-Morris, much longer; for the bare recollection of the tortures he had that day endured, were almost enough to force him to disclose what he knew.

He now tried to move his anguished body, and, after a while, felt some returning strength; the blood soon returned to those parts from which it had been excluded by the pressure of the weights that had been laid upon him, and though the anguish occasioned by it was great, yet the first violence of the pain being over, he gradually became more easy, and was soon able to partake of some of the coarse fare that lay beside him.

Weary with the late agitation he had undergone, a refreshing slumber now contributed to restore his exhausted strength; though, in his sleep, he still thought himself struggling under the pressure of the weights, and again, in the idea, endured the agonies of the past day.

When he awoke, he found himself so much recovered, as to be able to raise himself up on his hard bed; and he again endeavoured to add strength to his exhausted frame, by eating some of his provisions.

He found he had slept some time, as the sable mantle of night had completely enveloped the objects around him in murky darkness.

Nature seemed buried in profound repose—the sentinel at the door no longer vexed the solemn silence by his solitary paces— he too, perhaps wearied by long watching, had sunk in the still embraces of sleep; or, leaning on his battle spear, endeavoured to while away the tedious time, until relieved by his comrades, by recalling to his memory the past scenes of his youthful days, while his honest heart oft swelled at the recollection of some favourite companion, who, in the battle's heat, sunk by his side, oppressed by the chilly hand of Death, inflicted by the barbed arrow, or blood-stained glave.

CHAPTER XX.

"This is a gentle provost—Seldom when
The steeled gaoler is the friend of man."

SHAKESPEARE.

"Whither shall I fly?
Where hide me and my miseries together?
———I'm the wretchedest creature
E'er crawl'd on earth"

OTWAY.

WALTER, though with some difficulty, arose from his pallet of straw when the first beams of morning began to chase away the dark visions of night.

He immediately directed his steps to the grating in the roof, as that appeared to be the only way in which there was the slightest possibility of his effecting his escape. With an enquiring eye he examined it; the bars, however, were too firmly fixed in the stone-work to give him the slightest room to hope that his strength, now too that it was so much weakened, could remove them. Losing all hope, he turned away from the grating, and paced, with unequal and trembling steps, his dungeon.

The keeper of his dreary prison now made his appearance with the provisions; he seemed to be much surprised to find Walter able to walk, after what he had suffered the preceding day, and observed, that few men were able to bear the torture of the third weight for a moment, while he had not only bore it for a long time, but was able to move so soon after it.

Walter, encouraged by the man's entering into converse with him, began to lament the cruelty of his fate, which combined with human power to persecute an innocent man, whose only crime was that of wearing some clothes he had most unfortunately, and in an evil hour, bought of a pedlar, who, doubtless, had been concerned in the murder of Fitz-Morris.

The man seemed to be touched with compassion at his tale, and said, that he hoped that his innocence would appear plain to his lord, the Baron, on the following day; adding, that he being so partial to Fitz-Morris, who had, for a long series of years, been a tried and faithful steward to his large estate, made him more anxious, and the more strict, in endeavouring to find out the perpetrators of his murder, whom he, doubtless, would punish with every severity which the laws allowed him.

"Will you then," said Walter, "assist an innocent man, in making his escape from the unjust persecutions of your Lord, and who will amply repay your kindness?"

The man started back at the idea—"No," said he; "though you could fill your dungeon with gold, I would refuse it—I was born in this castle, I have lived in it more than forty years, and never yet betrayed a trust reposed in me. If you are innocent you need not fear, but, if you are guilty, your crime deserves the punishment you will doubtless receive."

So saying, the man left the dungeon, and Walter to the painful emotions excited by his last words.

The meridian sun now shone forth in all his powerful splendour, and Walter reflected that, ere that time to-morrow, he would be obliged to bear a renewal of the tortures so indelibly imprinted on his memory, and aching body. Driven to desperation by the tormenting idea, he seized hold of the grating, and endeavoured to shake it; the grate seemed to yield to his efforts, and some of the stone-work was soon much loosened that he was obliged to desist, for fear he should bring the whole down upon him.

Animated by the hope of delivering himself from the dangerous situation he was in, he now examined the stone-work around the sides, and, after some difficulty, got out a large piece, in which the iron bars had been fastened, but had been loosened from the cement that fixed them in, through time and his exertions: now that the bars were loose at one end, he easily pulled them out of the opposite stone-work, and, with sensations of delight, saw that he could easily effect his escape from the dungeon.

In this employ the hours passed away; night began to let fall her dusky curtain over the face of nature, and favoured his intent; he, however, impatiently waited until all around the castle was involved in darkness and silence, when, with some difficulty, he raised himself up, and emerging from his dungeon, found himself in a small court, completely covered with long waving grass.

Impatiently he looked around for an outlet, but, for a long time, saw no means of his getting out of the court. At last, a small postern attracted his notice; he approached it, and found it open; he entered into the gloomy space which appeared beyond it, and, meeting some steps, ventured to ascend them; he followed their winding course for some time, till gaining the summit, he found himself in a large corridor.

With an anxious palpitating heart, he cautiously paced to the end of the extensive passage; when, aided by the small remains of light that gleamed through the long Gothic windows, he discovered a large folding portal before him, one half of which was open; Walter entered, and had advanced some way, when, standing against the wall, near a large window, to his fear-struck eyes, he beheld the tall figure of a man.

His sensations, overcoming his faculties, denied him the power of leaving the spot he was standing on, and his strained eyes were riveted on the figure.

No movement, however, took place; and Walter, at last, gathering courage, advanced nearer to it, when, with joy, he found, that what he had suspected to be a man was only a coat of armour, of which he now saw many others ranged against the walls of the room, which appeared to be the armoury of the castle.

Walter now determined, as he saw no prospect of being able to make his escape that night, as he might, not knowing any way by which he could get out of the castle, endanger detection, to conceal himself, until the next evening, in one of the numerous coats of armour, as the safest plan he could pursue, to prevent being found out.

He accordingly attired himself in one; and, while he was so doing, the grey morning began to appear over the lofty summits of the battlements of the castle.

He was soon enabled to discern the objects around him, and found himself in a lofty chamber, or rather hall, hung round with innumerable coats of armour, pikes, spears, and swords; he looked through the windows on one side, and saw the same court into which he had arrived out of his dungeon; crossing the room, he gazed through the windows that were opposite, and perceived that they looked over the broad moat, and a wide extensive country.

He now retired to the place he had chosen—a dark corner, and which was filled up with coats of armour laid on each other without any order; in the midst of these, near the wall, he took his station, drawing several pieces around him, so that no part, except the helmet he wore, and which had its visor down, was perceptible.

He had not been long in this station, when the Baron entered, accompanied with several domestics.—"Allen," said he, speaking to one of them, "remove those coats of armour that are so negligently laid in yonder corner; let them be immediately cleaned, and placed up with the rest."

Allen bowed submissively to the Baron, and then ordered the domestics, who were with him, to commence the work.

Walter, whose ill stars had conducted him to this very corner, as a place of the greatest security he could find, could scarcely support his trembling frame, while he beheld the domestic busied about him, and expecting every moment to be discovered, and which must be the case, as soon as the armour was cleared away.

The Baron, who remained in the armoury viewing the workmen, directed them to remove some breastplates and cuirasses which Walter had piled up against himself; and one

of the servants had in his hand two of them which lay upper-
most, and which would have instantly discovered the upright
armour which covered his body, when the keeper of the dungeon
rushed hastily into the armoury, and, with a pallid countenance,
informed the Baron that the prisoner, who was supposed to be
the murderer of Fitz-Morris, had escaped out of his dungeon
through the grating which was in the roof.

The servants who were employed about the armour had
instantly stopped their labour, to hear what was the cause of the
agitation of the keeper; and immediately ran to the windows
which looked into the court, where the appearance of the grating
made it very plain that the man was correct in his relation.

The Baron, in the first ebullition of his rage, denounced
vengeance against the keeper and the sentinels, for their supposed
remissness in their duty.

He immediately ordered the domestics to leave their present
employ, and to endeavour to find out the place where the prisoner had concealed himself; since it was almost impossible that
he should have been able to effect his escape from the castle.

Walter, who had expected to have been discovered in a few
moments by the workmen, now began to feel a glow of hope,
occasioned by his present respite from the inevitable ruin that
appeared to be impending over him.

He saw the Baron quit the armoury with the domestics, and
proceed immediately to the court below, which they examined
all around; he heard them enter the door he had first perceived,
but, instead of ascending the stairs, they went to some other part
below, while their receding footsteps were soon lost to his attentive ears.

He, however, determined not to leave his present position,
as he now considered it the safest he could have, unless the
workmen again returned there; which, at least for that day,
seemed improbable, as they were all so intently engaged in
endeavouring to discover the place of his concealment.

CHAPTER XXI.

"A sudden storm did from the south arise;
And horrid black began to hang the skies;
By slow advances loaded clouds ascend,
And, 'cross the air, their low'ring fronts extend;
Heav'n's loud artillery began to play,
And wrath divine in dreadful peals convey;
Darkness, and raging winds, their terrors join,
And storms of rain with storms of fire combine."

BLACKMORE.

"He bound himself
To a strong mast, that liv'd upon the sea;
Where, like Arion on the dolphin's back,
I saw him hold acquaintance with the waves."

SHAKESPEARE.

WALTER now heard the steps of the Baron and his domestics pass along the passages below, as they were returning from their fruitless search; and he heard the Baron say, as he was ascending the stairs—"He could not have escaped, as I at first supposed, by the private postern below, which leads out on the moat, as you, Allen, say, you found it fastened within."

"Yes, my Lord," returned the other; "and, unless he has passed through the armoury, and hid himself in some of the turret-chambers above, it will be difficult to conceive where else he can be concealed."

These last words were spoken as they entered the armoury, which they immediately passed through, and ascended the stairs that led to the apartments above.

Having passed some time in their examination, they again came into the armoury, when Allen said—"Perhaps, my Lord, he has jumped into the moat through one of these windows, and, in that manner, effected his escape: it is the only way he can have gone, unless the sentinel betrayed his trust, which does not seem likely, as he certainly got out of his dungeon through the broken grating."

As Walter, when he was examining the situation of that part of the castle he was in, had opened the casement, and which he had left so, this last idea seemed to carry the greatest probability with it, and the Baron ordered his domestics to scour the country round, to endeavour to retake him.

Thus was Walter left once more to himself. In his plans for his escape, he treasured up in his memory the postern mentioned by the Baron as leading out on the moat, which was the very thing he wished to find; and, if he failed in that attempt, he determined to endeavour to get something to assist his descent from the window of the armoury into the moat, and so float himself over to the other side.

He saw no more of the Baron, or any other person, that day; and, with impatience; he waited in his covert, till the dusky twilight made it safe for him to emerge from it.

He now disencumbered himself from the armour, that had so well secured him from observation, and cautiously descending the steps, found, by the still feeble light, a long passage, with several others branching from it.

Walter took the one which, from its seeming direction, appeared to be that he wanted; nor was he mistaken, for, at the extremity of it, a door met his search—hastily he withdrew the bolts, when, at the bottom of a few steps, appeared the moat that surrounded the castle.

Walter for a long time surveyed the moat, which he was fearful to plunge in, for two reasons—the first was, that, as the moat was unusually broad, he doubted, in the weak state of his body, that he should be able to reach the opposite side; and the second reason was, that he was afraid the noise he should make in the water would call the attention of the sentinels; and, added to these, the opposite wall of the ditch was very high.

Walter was, however, too fertile in inventions, to fail in

contriving means for his escape; he went back into the armoury, and took from thence a grappling-iron, which he had observed the day before, and also some cordage, which he affixed to it; he then returned to the moat-grate, and, having, with great difficulty, raised it off its hinges, pushed it into the water, and, getting on it, soon floated over to the other side.

He now threw his grappling-iron on the wall, which, fixing with its crooked ends into the crevices where the stone-work was joined, he, with some difficulty, raised himself up, and was soon safe on the outside of the castle works.

Walter threw the grappling-iron into the moat, and then proceeded, as fast as he was able, from the walls of Manstow Castle.

Fear lent him wings, he forgot his bodily pains, and all that night did he proceed, uncertain whither he was going, only anxious to lengthen the distance between him and the Castle.

When the morning broke on him, he looked around, and saw that he was near the entrance of a large village; fearful of being seen, he turned on one side, and carefully avoided all appearance of habitations in his flight; at length, weary with fatigue, he lay down under the covert of a hedge, where he soon fell asleep.

Refreshed by his repose, he arose when the sun was beginning to decline behind the western hills, and continued his journey. As he now began to consider himself secure from all apprehensions of being taken, he resolved to enter a cottage which he saw near him, to obtain some refreshment. Having effected this, and obtained a direction to the sea-coast, he once more set out, and, without meeting any particular incident, arrived there.

Walter took up his residence at the cabin of a fisherman, and soon found an opportunity to be conveyed to the shores of Gallia in a small bark, which was then on the point of sailing.

He embarked in the evening, and waited, with anxiety, till the winds, which were veering about, should settle in the desired point. The mariners were equally impatient to begone as was Walter; for, the vessel being freighted with contraband articles, their delay was attended with much danger.

As soon, therefore, as the wind appeared in the least degree favourable, the swelling sails were unfurled to catch the breeze, the crooked anchor was raised from the sandy bottom, and soon the sea-girt shores of Albion diminished to the view, till, at length, they appeared like a cloud in the air, and shortly after were lost in obscurity.

As the wind was still contrary to their wishes, and encreased greatly in its violence, they were not able to make the desired shore, but were obliged to stand out farther to sea, and, by frequent tacking, to near as much as was possible the haven they were destined for.

The tempest now encreased so much, that the mariners, seeing not the least possibility of their being able to proceed on their voyage, directed their course back to the place they had sailed from.

The thunder now began to roll in tremendous peals along the vault of heaven, while the sulphurous lightning glared over the frothy billows, and presented an awful view of the deep, whose swelling surges, at times, raised the small vessel on their mountainous summits, and then dashed it down in their dark gulfs—frequently a huge sea would roll over the deck, and carry away every thing before it.

The rain poured down in torrents, and added to the horrors of the night; and the frequent, dreadful gusts of wind, howled dismally through the rigging of the vessel.

The mariners began to despair, and to give themselves up for lost. Walter, who stood upon the deck holding fast to the bending mast, viewed the tremendous scene before him with a fear-struck eye—in that awful situation, the remembrance of his crimes occurred to his tortured breast with tenfold sensations of agony, and he began to form resolutions of amending his life, when a black wave, rising over the side of the vessel, tore away the mast to which he had held, and carried him with it into the troubled deep.

Walter, however, quitted not his hold; and though the waves

rolled over him, and he was sometimes, for a long period, entombed in their briny bowels, yet he clung to the mast, well knowing that it was his only hope of preserving his existence.

Thus did he continue the whole night, struggling with the furious billows, and ignorant whither they were carrying him— from the moment he was washed into the sea, he had not seen the vessel, for the wave that tore the mast away, bore it in an instant far from the sight of the bark, or hearing of the cries of the hapless mariners.

At length the long wished-for day unveiled the horrors of the scene, and Walter, whose strength was almost exhausted, looked with a despairing eye around him, when he was elevated on a rolling billow, and, at a distance from him beheld, with indescribable emotions of joy, that he was fast approaching to a bold and rocky shore, on which he hoped to be saved from the watery grave that had so long opened her jaws to entomb him.

As he, however, advanced towards it, he began to fear that he should be dashed to pieces against the sharp craggy rocks that defended the coast. His fears were, however, dismissed, when he was carried by the rolling waves into a large bay.

The tremendous swell of the waters now began to abate, as he approached further up the bay; and, at length, the mast to which he had so long clung was washed upon the sands.

Walter, exerting his yet remaining strength, crawled up out of the reach of the restless waves, and sunk on the ground, insensible of feeling for the past horrors he had endured.

CHAPTER XXII.

"Ambition's like a circle on the water,
Which never ceases to enlarge itself,
Till, by broad spreading, it disperse to nought."

SHAKESPEARE.

"Why I can smile, and murder while I smile,
And cry content to that which grieves my heart,
And wet my cheeks with artificial tears,
And frame my face to all occasions."

SHAKESPEARE.

WHEN Walter recovered from the state of insensibility in which he had lain on the beach, unable longer to support the fatigue he had undergone, he cast his eyes around him, but could not tell what part of the world he was in.

With difficulty he raised himself from the ground, and staggered along the shore, in hopes of seeing some signs of "the busy haunts of men;" for a long time he looked in vain, but, at length, in a small valley, he beheld two or three straggling huts, and to them he directed his faint and languid steps.

Enquiring of the peasants, he found he had been thrown on the western shores of England, and that the recess in which he had been carried by the restless waves, was called the Bay of Tor.

He was now obliged to make use of the little money he had left (for he had paid for his passage beforehand), to procure him a few necessaries, and some clothes, as those he had on were tore to pieces in his struggling with the furious ocean.

Uncertain what he should in future do, for the present he took up his abode at a peasant's hut, in order to recruit his exhausted strength, and to fit him for his future undertakings.

In a few days he had quite recovered his fatigues, and, not

having any fears of being discovered in those remote parts, he
rambled about the adjacent country; but, instead of enjoying
the beauties of nature, which displayed themselves abundantly
around him, he would pass the time in ruminations on what
he should do, now that his money was expended, to obtain the
means of existence.

In one of these reveries he had strayed considerably beyond
his usual walk, and as he was going to return, the sounds of an
abbey clock broke on his ear, at no great distance.

Some thoughts now rushed into his mind, as the tolling bell
disturbed the silence around; and, guided by it, he directed his
steps towards the abbey.

Walter soon discovered the grey spires rising amidst the
surrounding forest; and now, from an opening in the wood, the
structure appeared to his view. It was situated in a beautiful part
of the country, with a spacious lawn before it; on one side, a
stream meandered through the adjoining meadows, encreasing,
by its gentle waves, their rich verdure. The banks were thickly
lined with trees, and, as the sun pierced their gloomy shades, it
sparkled, in reflected brilliance, on the bosom of the stream.

The abbey was built in a quadrangular form, and was of
great extent, its western front commanding a fine bold prospect;
and, from the extreme height of the turrets, which towered far
above the lofty oaks, an unconfined view was obtained of all the
surrounding scenery, rich in varied beauty, and romantic wildness.
From this could also be seen the spacious Bay of Tor, receiving,
in its ample bosom, the rolling waves of the vast Atlantic, whose
beauteous shores were clothed with luxuriant verdure, where
peace and contentment seemed to dwell.

As he approached the abbey, he heard the monks chaunting
the evening vespers; reminded by this of the lateness of the hour,
he hastened back to the miserable hut in which he had taken his
abode.

It occurred to him that he could not do any thing better, in his
present situation, than to retire to a monastery, where there was

little fear that he would ever be discovered, and which he could leave whenever it suited his inclination. At the time, indeed, there appeared nothing else that he could do, his pecuniary resources being quite exhausted.

When the lark, soaring high in the vaulted arch of heaven, tuned his morning hymn to the Creator of the Universe, Walter arose from his hard pallet, and directed his steps towards the abbey, which his host informed him was called by the name of Ford.

In his way he framed a tale, such as he thought would be best suited to raise the compassion of the holy fathers, and to effect his present purpose of being admitted as a lay-brother into the monastery.

When he arrived at the abbey, he begged to be conducted to the presence of the abbot or superior; before whom, affecting a piety, and total disregard of the world, which was far from his heart, he begged to be admitted within the blessed walls, where alone he should find ease from the oppressions of the world.

The good abbot, who believed all he said, began to feel for him a brotherly affection, and granted his wish.

Walter had not been long within the walls, before he began to perceive that, even in these retirements, he might make use of those arts with which nature had so liberally endowed him; he, therefore, put on a most rigid conduct with respect to his religious exercises, was frequent in his voluntary penances, and, in other respects, conducted himself in so exemplary a manner, that he obtained leave of the abbot to take the monastic vows, long before the customary year was expired.

Father Bertrand, for that was the name he had assumed on entering the monastery, was now become famous round the country for his piety. But the hopes of obtaining the elevated chair was the spur of all his actions; that was now become the summit of his ambition, and which he incessantly laboured, by his well-feigned actions, which outwardly appeared to have religion only for their motive, to obtain.

He no sooner heard that it was in the gift of the possessor of the domain of Berry Pomeroy Castle, than he sought all opportunities of assisting at the performance of mass in the Castle chapel, and a thousand times wished he was able to remove the venerable Father Oswald, in hopes of being appointed to the situation himself. He saw Sir Hugh de Pomeroy was greatly attached to the Father, and was fearful that, should the present abbot die, he would be appointed to that situation; he began, however, to entertain some hopes, when Sir Hugh died, that he might be able to influence the Lady Matilda de Pomeroy in his favour; but in this he was disappointed; nevertheless he did not fail, but rather encreased in his outward religious deportment, which had gained him so much reputation.

When he was appointed confessor to the Lady Elinor de Pomeroy, he began to think he had got up one step of the ladder which would raise him to the summit of his wishes; which he saw verified by her ambitious views, and which he hesitated not to assist by schemes the most diabolical; though, in every thing he did, he acted in such a wary and circumspect manner, that, even were it discovered, the blame would in no wise attach itself to him; and, even should there be a suspicion that he was concerned, he well knew his reputed sanctity of manners would serve as a veil to his actions, beneath which they would be scarce perceptible; and, in the mean time, by his acquiescence to the wishes of the Lady Elinor, he made himself certain of attaining the elevation he so much desired.

Thus have we detailed the adventures of Walter, or rather Henry Fitz-Auburne, to the period when he was first noticed in our history. When our readers have reviewed his past life, they will not wonder at his consenting to the nefarious and horrible scheme, of the taking off of the Lady Matilda de Pomeroy, since she presented an insurmountable bar to his ambitious projects.

It will appear, also, that he was too deeply plunged in deeds of blood to be longer disturbed by his conscience; for the mind, at last, becomes familiar to guilt, and what at first it would start at with horror, at length, by frequent repetition, it becomes completely callous to.

Such was Father Bertrand, who had, by his dark plans, obtained the dignified situation of superior, or abbot of Ford, after he had been but a few short years at the abbey, solely by dint of dissimulation and acts of villainy. Wrapt up in security, he little dreamt of a day of retribution for his numerous offences; and, in his heart, disowned that great Creator of the universe, whom, in public, he seemed to adore, and to dedicate his whole life to.

We shall now proceed with a detail of the actions of the Lady Elinor de Pomeroy, having unfolded to the reader the life and character of her counselor and abettor, the abbot Bertrand, who, to feed his insatiable avarice, was still her agent in her dark designs. He was perfectly conscious how much he had her in his power, and neglected not to make the greatest use of that knowledge. His behaviour, however, was the same as before, fawning and submissive; but under it lurked every baneful passion that ever dwelt in the breast of a human being, but which he well knew how to controul, and render invisible to the most sharp-sighted observer.

CHAPTER XXIII.

"Mad with her anguish, impotent to bear
The mighty grief, she loaths the vital air;
She raves against the gods, she beats her breast,
And tears, with trembling hands, her sable vest."

DRYDEN.

"Spirits, in what shape they chuse,
Dilated or condens'd, bright or obscure,
Can execute their airy purposes,
And works of love or enmity fulfil."

MILTON.

THE Lady Elinor de Pomeroy, in the departure of De Clifford, saw a termination to the faint hope that had, till now, existed, of an union with him. Her grief and inward laments soon began to produce a change in her tortured frame, and which the following circumstance tended greatly to encrease.

One evening, as she was sitting indulging her melancholy ruminations in her chamber, when the shades of evening had enveloped every object around in their dusky gloom, involun-tarily she sighed out the name of De Clifford. "Most beloved of men," said she, "would that I could look into the dark bosom of futurity, and there learn if it will ever be my happy lot to possess thee. Alas! but for thee, I might now have still been guiltless of a sister's blood; and, though not the inheritress of these proud towers, yet I should have felt far more content, and more peace of mind, than now I can ever hope for. O, happy Matilda, if thou couldst see the sorrows of thy sister, even thou, wronged as thou art, would pity her!"

"I do pity, and pray Heaven to forgive thee," replied slowly a faint well-known voice; and the affrighted Elinor, looking up, saw, standing near her, the pale wan form of the sainted

114

Matilda—her senses were on the point of forsaking her, when, ere they had quite departed, the spirit uttered these words:

"Think not, hope not, to possess the ill-fated De Clifford, who now is entombed in the merciless waves—his blood rests on thee, the cause of so much woe. Think that there is an eternity, and prepare thyself——"

Elinor heard no more, but, shrieking wildly, sunk, overpowered with fear and horror, lifeless on the ground.

When she opened her eyes, she found herself in the arms of her women, and Father Bertrand, now the abbot, standing by her—"O heavens!" she exclaimed, "I have seen her!—I have heard her voice!—she has accused me with the blood of De Clifford, who is no more."

"Heaven preserve your fleeting senses!" said the Abbot—"who have you seen?"

"Oh, yes," said Elinor, wildly; "'tis true I have seen her, I have seen the shade of Matilda."

"Of Matilda!" said the Abbot, his countenance assuming a pale and deadly cast; "suffer me, Lady, to bid your domestics leave the chamber, while I commune with you on the vision which has so disturbed your senses."

Elinor motioned to the women to retire; and, when they had quitted the apartment, the Abbot drew from her a recital of the supernatural appearance; and, when she had informed him of every circumstance, he arose from his seat, and paced the chamber in great agitation. At last, turning to the Lady Elinor, he said—"Your mind, Lady, is so disturbed, that you conceive these visions are built on reality; to-morrow I will commune with you more largely on this subject; the night is now far advanced—farewell, Lady, the saints take you in their holy keeping."

So saying, he immediately departed, and the domestics re-entering, the Lady Elinor retired, with a mind agitated by the recent events, to her couch.

When she arose the next morning, the first news she heard was, that the vessel in which De Clifford had sailed, when he left the kingdom, had been attacked by some Italian pirates, and that he had perished in the engagement.

Although she had endeavoured to persuade herself that the appearance she had seen the preceding evening was only in her mind's eye, yet this dreadful news was too evidently a confirmation, that the inanimate shade of her murdered sister still wandered on the earth; and the music she had heard some time back, now occurred to her distracted imagination; and, for a long period, she looked the silent image of despair.

Even the attentions and conversation of the Abbot failed in their customary effects of ameliorating her grief—De Clifford, the idol of her heart, was no more; he, for whom she had committed such foul crimes, in order to possess his love, was gone, and life itself, although her ambitious views, in possessing the domains of Berry Pomeroy, had met with success, was become a tedious burthen.

At length time restored her to her former tranquillity of mind, and, as the Abbot predicted, the deeds she had been guilty of, when viewed at a distance, lost the terrific appearance which they assumed when at first she beheld them on their perpetration. Even the remembrance of De Clifford was now become but as the vision of the night, which fades at the approach of dawn, or only leaves an uncertain recollection behind.

The beauties of her person brought to the Castle of Berry Pomeroy many brave knights, who sighed at the shrine of her charms.

Amongst the most conspicuous of these was Sir Hugh de Seymour, and Sir Ethelred de Fortebrand, both men of considerable interest in the court, and possessed of great riches.

Sir Hugh de Seymour was of an ardent disposition, hating controul; his capacities were great, his resolutions were quickly formed; at one glance he could discover the secret springs that set a plot in motion, and, as suddenly, he could devise means to counteract the scheme. He was of a commanding figure, an impressive countenance, and seemed formed for great enterprizes.

Sir Ethelred de Fortebrand, on the other hand, added to an interesting figure, was possessed of a great share of duplicity, and was of a designing disposition; his countenance never betrayed the secret workings of his heart; he could hold a conversation with, and profess a friendship for the very man, whom, perhaps, the moment before he had hired an assassin to destroy.

Of all the numerous suitors for her hand, the Lady Elinor seemed most to favour the addresses of Sir Hugh de Seymour, and De Fortebrand soon perceived the particular attention she paid to him. He saw in him a rival not to be despised, and was now become his bitter enemy.

De Seymour daily encreased in the good graces of the Lady Elinor, and it was generally supposed throughout the Castle, that he would soon be the lord of it.

In proportion as he encreased in the favourable opinion of the Lady Elinor, De Fortebrand apparently relaxed in his addresses, as if perceiving that De Seymour was the fortunate lover, he had given up all hopes, and now visited the Lady Elinor but as an acquaintance.

By this conduct he entirely deceived the unsuspecting De Seymour, who, no longer looking upon him as a rival, received him into his friendship, which Fortebrand with industry cultivated. Their mornings, except those on which De Seymour dedicated to the Lady Elinor, were generally passed together, either in the hunt, or in viewing the beauties of the neighbouring country.

It was during these periods, when De Fortebrand appeared all openness, candour, and sincerity, that he was inwardly brooding schemes of a black and horrible nature, by which he might rid himself of the hated De Seymour; and then, he thought there was little doubt but that he would soon prevail on the Lady Elinor to grant to him her hand, which he longed to possess for more than one reason.

Her great fortune was no inconsiderable spur to his designs, for, though he was supposed to have large possessions, yet, being greatly addicted to gaming, he had, of late, considerably impoverished his estates, and her fortune would amply suffice to recruit his exhausted finances, and afford him the means of pursuing his darling gratifications; and, in addition to this, he was far from being insensible to the commanding beauties of her fine person.

He soon contrived to insinuate himself into the confidence of De Seymour, from whom he learnt, that he had every reason to suppose his addresses to the Lady Elinor de Pomeroy were favourably received; and that, in a short time, he hoped he should be the happy possessor of her charming person.

Fortebrand affected to listen to the expressions of De Seymour's delight, and the happiness he prognosticated to himself, with apparent composure, and even congratulated him on his success, as if, having given up all idea of Lady Elinor himself, he no longer viewed De Seymour as a rival: and the enamoured De Seymour, feeling a satisfaction in communicating his expected happiness to one, from whose conduct he thought he could apprehend no danger in supplanting him in the affections of Elinor, daily encreased in his expressions of friendship and esteem for him; little thinking what passions of dark and dreadful natures were hid in the breast of De Fortebrand, who now impatiently waited for an opportunity to effect his horrible purposes, by which he hoped to rid himself of a hated rival, and gain the hand of the Lady Elinor, and the extensive domains attached to Berry Pomeroy Castle.

CHAPTER XXIV.

"Such is the fate of guilt, to make slaves tools,
And then to make them masters by our secrets."

HAVARD.

"Behold a cliff, whose high and bending head
Looks dreadful down upon the warring deep:
How fearful,
And dizzy, 'tis to cast one's eyes so low!
The crows and choughs, that wing the midway air,
Shew scarce so gross as beetles."

SHAKESPEARE.

THE coast, on the western side of the Bay of Tor, terminates in a lofty rock, the end of which rises perpendicularly from the ocean. From the summit of this rock, on a clear day, the view is extremely beautiful.

Below, on the left, are seen the tall vessels at anchor; and the busy cries of the seamen, preparing to depart, or hailing their comrades, who, with blithesome hearts, have just arrived from some distant shore, and well pleased survey their well-known native coast, are heard. From these objects the eye rests, with delight, on the opposite side of the Bay, whose romantic hills, covered with rich verdure, and the fleecy tribe, who wander delighted over the luxuriant pastures, present a view capable of tranquillizing, for a time, the sorrows of the heart.

To the right, are seen the immeasurable waters of the vast Atlantic, over whose tumultuous bosom the vessels are seen gliding, till they are hid by its intervening waves.

De Seymour was particularly delighted with this view, and he would frequently ride there with Fortebrand, to enjoy the cool refreshing breeze from off the boundless waves of the vast Atlantic.

This was the spot which De Fortebrand pitched on for the accomplishment of his fell purposes, as it was far from any habitation, and appeared well calculated for his intents.

He well knew, that if he was seen riding with De Seymour on the same day that he was missing, some suspicion would naturally rest on him; he, therefore, gave out, that he was unwell, and confined himself, for a time, to his house, which was on the borders of the romantic Dart.

At the end of the grounds which lay at the back of his house, was a gate, which opened near a path which wound along the sea-shore, and by which he could, at any time, go to that place unobserved. He, therefore, secretly repaired there every morning, in expectation of seeing De Seymour, who he knew frequently visited the spot, to enjoy the cool breeze, and the beautiful view.

On the third morning he beheld his intended victim riding up, and went forwards to meet him. De Seymour seemed surprised to find Fortebrand there, who accounted for it by observing, that he had strolled so far, seduced by the uncommon beauty of the morning, to inhale the refreshing sea air.

De Seymour now dismounted from his horse, which he turned loose to graze, and walked along near the edge of the precipice with De Fortebrand, conversing on the subject that so much occupied his mind, namely, the hopes he entertained of his union with the Lady Elinor.

Fortebrand suddenly stopped, and remarking that he saw a fish of an unusual size in the sea, leant over the precipice as if watching it. De Seymour, impelled by his curiosity, did the same, and, while in that attitude, Fortebrand, getting behind him, pushed him over the rocky edge.

De Fortebrand waited a few moments, and then heard the body of the unfortunate De Seymour dash into the waves below. Well convinced that his rival was now for ever removed, he, with cautious steps, stole away from the place, and unobserved, save by Him before whose eyes our most secret transactions appear, gained the grounds which were attached to his mansion.

When De Seymour was found not to return at his usual hour to his residence, his domestics made the most minute enquiries after him. Supposing that he might have been at the mansion of De Fortebrand, they repaired to it, but was informed that he had not been there for some days.

At Berry Pomeroy Castle no information could be gained of him—he had not been there that day. His usual rides were then traced, and his horse being found on the grounds near the precipice, it was conjectured that he must have fallen from it into the sea; and, in a few days, that idea was confirmed, by his body being found on the opposite side of the bay, whither the waves had borne it.

De Fortebrand, during this period, pretended to be still afflicted with indisposition, and even kept his bed, to carry on the deceit. He also affected to be greatly grieved with the loss of his dear friend, for so he termed De Seymour.

As De Fortebrand was supposed not to have stirred from his mansion for some time previous to the death of Sir Hugh de Seymour, it was impossible for the smallest breath of suspicion to rest on him. In secret, therefore, he congratulated himself on the success that had attended his diabolical schemes.

As soon as he judged it proper, he left his mansion, and paid a visit to the Lady Elinor de Pomeroy, who appeared to receive him with more than usual attention, nor scarcely once mentioned, during their conversation, the name of De Seymour.

Fortebrand was secretly pleased with this circumstance, because it evidently shewed that he had not proceeded far in her estimation, and that there was the greater probability his sanguine ideas might be realized.

The fact was, that De Fortebrand had ever been the greatest favourite with the Lady Elinor, but De Seymour's large estates turned the balance in his favour; and, now that he was gone, she again looked with the eye of partiality on De Fortebrand, whose possessions were supposed but little inferior to De Seymour's.

Such was Lady Elinor, whose heart, that had been devoted

so much to De Clifford, now that he was no more, unable to love another object, was solely bent on ambitious designs to aggrandize herself.

Fortebrand soon profited by the favourable opinion he saw the Lady Elinor entertained for him, and soon received her consent to an alliance, which the Abbot Bertrand, whom she had consulted on the subject, persuaded her to do; for De Fortebrand, from whose scrutinizing eyes nothing could be hid, saw the great influence the Abbot had over the Lady Elinor, and, knowing his greedy and avaricious disposition, secretly visited him, and, amongst other things, promised to cede to him the lands appertaining to the Abbey, and also that edifice itself, as soon as he, the Abbot Bertrand, should have prevailed on the Lady Elinor de Pomeroy to grant him her hand, by which he would become the possessor of that estate.

It may be easily supposed, from what our readers know of the character of the Abbot, that this kind of rhetoric was not lost on him; such a proceeding would render him secure in his present situation, and, in fact, was the very thing he had anxiously wished to possess. He knew that the Lady Elinor's avaricious disposition never would have granted it to him, unless he disclosed some circumstances to her known only to himself, but which might, in the end, overwhelm him in ruin.

This was too dangerous an undertaking for his wary policy; and he, therefore, listened, with much satisfaction, to the offers of De Fortebrand, and promised to exert his influence with the Lady Elinor, to consent to an alliance with him.

This he soon effected, by representing to Elinor that the possessions of De Fortebrand were sufficient, when joined with her's, to sate rapacity itself, and that certain tales that had gone forth, respecting the involvement of his circumstances, were raised only by the partisans of De Seymour, whose interest it was to promulgate them, that he might the easier attain her hand.

The Lady Elinor listened with attention to the discourse of the artful Abbot, and, at length, as the reader is informed, gave her consent, and a day was appointed for the nuptials.

De Fortebrand, transported with the success of his plans, embraced the Abbot, reminding him of the promise he had made of the grant of the abbey and lands, and which, as soon as he possessed them, he would ratify to him.

Thus was the Lady Elinor completely become the tool of him, whom, at first, she considered entirely as an implement of her own. By making him the confident of her guilty deeds, he soon gained an entire ascendancy over her.

The proud banners which waved with the breeze from the lofty turrets of Berry Pomeroy Castle, shewed the day arrived which was to give it a lord.

Soon a numerous train was seen winding over the hills, and De Fortebrand appeared, mounted on a superb courser, in the midst of the cavalcade.

The banners of his house were borne in front; then followed twenty domestics, having his arms on the sleeve of their doublets; next were two trumpeters; then followed two pages, bearing his shield and helmet, preceding De Fortebrand; after him, followed twenty more domestics, habited in like manner as their fellows in front; and, after them, a long train of menials and retainers.

The numerous retinue halted before the gates of the Castle, when the trumpeters blew a blast, which was answered from its walls. The drawbridge then slowly descended, and over it Forte- brand proceeded, amidst rows of the domestics of the Castle, who bowed lowly as he passed: dismounting, he advanced into the great hall, at the upper end of which, on a throne, appeared the Lady Elinor de Pomeroy, surrounded by her female attend- ants, elegantly attired, and by her side the Abbot Bertrand.

As soon as De Fortebrand had advanced into the centre of the hall, the Lady Elinor descended from her throne, and, slowly bending before him, welcomed him to the castle, and then motioned him to seat himself beside her. The band of music then struck up, and made the hall echo with their martial notes.

The Abbot now descended from his seat, and advanced

towards the Castle chapel, followed by De Fortebrand holding
the Lady Elinor's hand; after them walked two priests, who were
to assist, and then the female attendants, two and two. Next
came the vassals and retainers of De Fortebrand; and, after them,
the retainers of the Lady Elinor.

As soon as the whole train was assembled in the chapel, the
Abbot Bertrand performed the marriage ceremony; which was
no sooner ended, than the trumpets blew a cheerful blast, and
the banners which waved on the battlements of the Castle were
taken down, and others, in which the arms of De Fortebrand
were quartered with those of the Pomeroys, hoisted in their stead.

The train then returned in the same order to the hall, where a
magnificent collation had, in the interim, been prepared.

CHAPTER XXV.

"He found his veins with indignation swell,
    And felt within the fire and rage of hell;
    Legions of spleenful spirits fill'd his breast,
    And dire revenge his troubled soul possess'd."

                              BLACKMORE.

"Disdain and scorn ride sparkling in her eyes,
    Despising what they look on."

                              SHAKESPEARE.

THUS was, at length, concluded the marriage between Sir
Ethelred de Fortebrand and the Lady Elinor de Pomeroy,
through the assistance of the Abbot Bertrand; who, some few
weeks after, finding that Sir Ethelred did not make good his
promises, in ceding to him his promised reward, for his inter-
posing in his behalf with the Lady Elinor, of the Abbey of Ford,
and the domains attached to it, began to fear, that now De
Fortebrand had so well succeeded in his plans, he would neglect
those who had assisted him in them.

For this surmise he had, indeed, great reason, as Sir Ethelred, soon perceiving the rapacious disposition of his consort, was fearful of making any mention to her of such a gift being his intention, lest it should draw from her an investigation into the reasons which induced him to bestow it, and also an enquiry into his own affairs and circumstances, out of which he could easily, had what he advanced concerning them been true, have made a handsome requital for any services the Abbot might have rendered him.

He, therefore, determined to put off the Abbot, with promises of his intention to perform what now he secretly never meant to do; and he was not ignorant that the Abbot, and his train of monks, owed to him the homage of vassalage, as residing on his estate; and, should the Abbot be disposed to demand the performance of his promise, he would, in that case, explain to him the situation in which he stood, and the tributary homage he should require.

The Abbot, once so placed, nothing but ecclesiastical power could remove; and Bertrand was too cautious to allow the smallest imputation to be made against his religious deportments, and warily kept himself secure from the envenomed shafts of malice, for he well knew that his arbitrary conduct, and strict rule over the inhabitants of the Abbey, had not made him any friends; and he knew too much of the world, and of himself, to believe that the few who fawned on him with servile adulation, did it for any other purpose than to gain their own ends, and would, in all probability, should there be culpability in any shape attached to him, turn out his most bitter enemies.

Bertrand judged of mankind by himself, and that it was made him so cautious; he, however, determined to seek a conference with Sir Ethelred, and then to remind him of his promise.

As he was so frequently at the Castle, a convenient opportunity soon occurred; and, finding him alone in his chamber, he approached him with affected humility.

"Save you, my Lord," said he, "the saints preserve you in their holy keeping."

"And you too, holy Father," returned De Fortebrand; "and be your prayers heard.—Is there aught, Father, I can do to serve our holy church? Comest thou its suppliant, or to refresh my ears with thy persuasive eloquence?"

"I come, my Lord, a suppliant for it and myself," replied the Abbot; "my Lord, the Baron, it is likely, may recollect the promise made to me of a grant of the Abbey and domains to the poor servants of its holy walls, who, in their grateful orisons, will ever remember the bounteous gift."

"Thou hast indeed rightly judged of my recollection, Father," returned De Fortebrand, "but there are some bars to the immediate attainment of thy wishes; nor can I, at this early season of my alliance with the Lady Elinor, in strict propriety take those steps which, at some future period, may more discreetly be done."

"Heaven rest our souls!" piously returned the Abbot, crossing himself, "our wants are few indeed; in our religious exercises, and the adornment of our holy chapel and shrines of our blessed saints, pass away our lives; but the poor inhabitants of Ford want the means to render that outward appearance of devotion and respect which is so deeply engraven in their hearts—it is now three months since at the altar I joined your hand with the Lady Elinor's in holy bond, and perhaps my Lord may still think well of the request of the humble servant of the church."

De Fortebrand now began to perceive that the Abbot was not to be so easily put off as he had hoped he would be, and he was greatly enraged to find, after what he had said, he still persisted in his request.

"I tell thee, Father," said he, "it suits me not at present to comply with the promise made to thee previous to my marriage; and it doth not a little astonish me, Father, that you, who so cheaply hold the abbey and its lands, which for many years I find hath not paid its accustomed dues to the possessors of the domain, should complain of poverty, when, it is well known, your coffers are well stored with the munificence of the inhabitants of this castle."

"I advance not, my Lord, what is untrue," returned the Abbot, who now plainly saw that Sir Ethelred had no idea of performing his promise, and which stung his malicious soul to the quick, to think he should thus have been so completely his dupe; "the servants of the church know not the language of untruth, falsehood dwelleth not among them, nor are our coffers stored with the munificence of the possessors of these towers."

"Re-echo not back my words, Abbot," returned Sir Ethelred de Fortebrand, in a voice almost choked with rage; "it ill becomes a servant of the church to possess so much greedy rapacity, or for a dependant to dictate to his lord."

"A dependant!" returned the Abbot, equally infuriated with passion, and, for a moment, forgetting his accustomed caution; "the ministers of the church, my Lord, are dependant on no one but the bright heavenly host they serve; and, when applied to an earthly power, save his holiness the Pope, they both scorn and disclaim the words."

"Say you so, Abbot," replied Sir Ethelred, with rage gleaming in his eyes, "then mark my words—know that to me belong the abbey and domains, and, by the powers above, I swear, that if on the day after the morrow thou comest not with thy canting train to pay me my right of homage and vassalage for the same, thou and thy followers exist not another night beneath its lofty roofs—look to it well, for such is my fixed resolve."

So saying, with rage and indignation in his face, he quitted the apartment, and left the Abbot transfixed to the spot on which he stood, by the variety of contending emotions which warred within his breast, and left him incapable of action. So terrible a blow to his pride he had little dreamt of, nor knew he how to avoid it—if he went to the Lady Elinor concerning it, the secret of his having listened to the application of Sir Ethelred, to apply to the Lady Elinor in favour of her alliance with De Fortebrand, and of his having agreed so to do, and the promised bribe that he was to receive, could not long remain a secret, and which might weaken his interest with her; on the other hand, his pride could not support the humiliating idea of paying De Fortebrand homage, and any thing appeared better that would hinder such a degrading circumstance from taking place; he, therefore, was determined to run all hazard, to be freed from the servile obedience he was ordered to render to Sir Ethelred, as his right as lord of the domain.

He, therefore, sent to a domestic to the Lady Elinor de Fortebrand, to beg a converse with her on a momentous business, and was immediately ushered to her apartment.

"What is the matter, holy Father?" said Lady Elinor; "why is such sorrow depicted in thy features? unfold, I pray you, the cause of your grief."

"Fair daughter," said the Abbot, "the humiliation I have but now undergone, is a sufficient cause that my whole frame should be convulsed with sorrow—thou too, Lady, art concerned, inasmuch as the high office I now hold, and which was given me by thee, has been treated with indignity."

"For heaven's sake, Father, name the cause, and Elinor will give thee ample satisfaction for thy injuries."

"Sorry am I to say, Lady, the cause is best known to Sir Ethelred, for he it is who has ordered me to attend in this castle, with my train of holy brethren, to pay him homage and vassalage for the possession and tenantry of Ford Abbey; and ill it accords with the high office of Religion that her servants should bend the knee to laical authority."

"And can it be possible, Father," said the Lady Elinor, "that Fortebrand could so far forget you and myself, as to issue such a mandate! but rest thee awhile here, holy Father, while I seek Sir Ethelred, and persuade him to revoke an order which much astonisheth me."

The Abbot bowed lowly to the Lady Elinor, who arose from her seat, and left the apartment. Now was the moment of trial, for, should De Fortebrand explain his errand, the Lady Elinor would, doubtless, conceive anger against him, for her ambition and rapacity could only be equalled by his; but, on the other hand, he reflected, that, by so doing, De Fortebrand would equally expose himself, and this idea gave him great hopes that he would let the transaction rest in oblivion. He saw, with much pleasure, that the Lady Elinor appeared greatly enraged at Sir Ethelred's degrading order, and he was in great hopes that she would procure a countermand of it.

The Lady Elinor proceeded immediately to the apartments of Sir Ethelred, to which he had again returned. The passion which had been agitated by the converse of the abbot had not, as yet, subsided; and Lady Elinor saw, as, lowly bending, she approached him, the conflict which raged within; determined, however, to gain her point, she thus addressed him:

"I come, my Lord," said she, "a suppliant for myself and the holy abbot of Ford—a suppliant for myself, in regard to my having instated him in the high office he holds, and which it would ill become me to have degraded; and also to entreat, on his part, that you will not oblige him, who holds the high office of abbot, to pay homage to you."

"Sorry am I to say, your request, Lady Elinor, cannot, in this instance, be complied with, and my orders shall be obeyed, or let him look to the consequence—your further converse on this head is useless—I am fixed in my resolves."

"What, Sir Ethelred," said the enraged Elinor, "are the entreaties of your wife of so little avail?"

"Even so, in this instance, Lady Elinor," said the Baron, with a provoking calmness.

"And you are determined that the abbot of Ford, and the holy fathers of that community, shall pay you homage, as living on the domains attached to Berry Pomeroy, an act as yet without precedent?"

"Yes, Lady Elinor," replied Sir Ethelred; "I am most irrevocably determined that he shall, or that day the roofs of the abbey shall cease to cover him and his fraternity."

"Then mark the consequence," haughtily returned the Lady Elinor; and indignantly disdaining further converse, arose from her seat and left the chamber, and immediately proceeded to her apartment, to relate the ill success of her application to the Abbot.

CHAPTER XXVI.

"Come, ye spirits
That tend on mortal thoughts, unsex me here;
And fill me, from the crown to the toe, top full
Of direst cruelty! make thick my blood,
Stop up the access and passage to remorse,
That no compunctious visitings of nature
Shake my fell purpose, nor keep peace between
The effect and it!"

SHAKESPEARE.

As the Abbot rose up to receive the Lady Elinor on her return from Sir Ethelred, he observed her countenance flushed with anger, and, from her agitated appearance, prognosticated that she had met with a contemptuous refusal.

"Father," said she hastily, and vainly endeavouring to conceal the violence of her emotions, "I have not succeeded; Sir Ethelred has treated my request with scorn, and you must undergo the penance—but be content to do it, for both you and myself shall have ample vengeance."

Thus saying, she seated herself, and tried to recover from her great agitation. Her pride was hurt, she had been foiled in her application, and sensations of deadly hatred and revenge arose in her bosom, and completely erased whatever sparks of affection there might have been for De Fortebrand.

The Abbot, seeing the state of mind she was in, endeavoured to encrease the breach that he had been the occasion of between her and her lord.

"Lady," said he, "happy should I indeed be if this circumstance is the only one in which you may have reason to be offended with Sir Ethelred, but, I fear, there are other matters of a heavier nature that will soon appear against him, and tend to blacken his now fair fame in your eyes."

"What is it, holy Father, you allude to?" said the Lady Elinor —"speak—satisfy me in what more I shall have reason to regret my union with De Fortebrand."

"When I was first acquainted with Sir Ethelred," said the insidious monk, "I learnt from every one that his estates and possessions were great, and free from all incumbrances, that his character was that of an honest man; but within this last month, Lady, sorry am I to be the bearer of such ill news, I have understood that his circumstances are greatly involved, that the shadow of his former property is all he now possesses, the incomes arising from his estates being applied to pay immense debts he has contracted; and that, had he not been so fortunate as to ally himself to you, he must, ere this, have wandered a wretched exile from his native shore."

"And is this true, Father?" said Elinor; "have you good authority for what you have advanced?"

"Daughter," said the Abbot, in an affected solemn tone, "it is as true as that there is a power above."

For a while inarticulate rage possessed the whole frame of the Lady Elinor—one while her cheeks were dyed with a crimson tint, at another moment they were blanched and appeared of a livid hue; her body shook with passion, her hands were clenched, her eyes fixed, and her mouth was open; her lips moved, but no utterance came forth, and her breath was short and convulsed.

The Abbot, seated at a distance from the Lady Elinor, with his arms folded, and his head declined, secretly watched the transitions of her furious rage with indescribable pleasure; he, indeed, saw clearly that he should have ample vengeance, for he well knew what she was capable of performing, from past experience.

He waited till she appeared somewhat to have recovered, and then arose, saying—"Daughter, I shall now leave you; the servile task I have to perform on the day after the morrow, in the hall of this castle, will need some preparation. Farewell, Lady, the saints preserve you in their holy keeping."

"And you too, Father," said the Lady Elinor.—"Farewell—let

me see you after the degrading task you have to perform—
remember Elinor is your friend, and that vengeance is awake."

The Abbot bowed low, and departed to the Abbey; and the
next morning, having convened the monks, he informed them
of the imperious orders of Sir Ethelred, and that they must, on
the morrow, proceed to the Castle of Berry Pomeroy, to pay the
homage of vassalage for the lands of the Abbey of Ford, which
belonged to the domain of the Castle.

Although the fathers well knew that the lord of the manor had
a right to demand their homage, yet, as it was a circumstance that
never had occurred before in their recollections, they felt averse to
the task; but the Abbot informed them, that, in case they refused
to comply, they would no longer be allowed to remain in the
sanctified walls where many of them had passed nearly the whole
of their lives, and that he must swallow the bitter pill, though
greatly averse to it; he, therefore, gave the necessary directions,
and then dismissed the brethren, who retired discontented to
their cells.

The next morning the Abbot, having convened the fraternity,
proceeded from forth the grey walls of Ford, towards the Castle
of Berry Pomeroy.

First walked a bare-headed friar, carrying a crucifix; after him
came the abbot, in the rich dress of his station, supported by two
friars, also bare-headed; then next followed the fathers, two and
two; and, after them, the lay-brethren.

In this manner the train wound along the road, till they came
in front of the grand gate of Berry Pomeroy Castle; there they
stopped, and solemnly chaunted a hymn; they then proceeded
over the drawbridge, and advanced into the great hall.

Here, on a throne of state, sat Sir Ethelred de Fortebrand,
surrounded by the officers of his household, all in their richest
liveries, bearing on their sleeves the arms of the De Fortebrands
and De Pomeroys quartered.

When the train had advanced into the hall, one of De Fortebrand's heralds exclaimed—"Whence come ye?"

"From the Abbey of Ford," replied the first monk, "to pay homage to the most noble Sir Ethelred de Fortebrand, lord of the domain."

"Advance then," returned the herald, "and bend the knee, in token of your vassalage, before Sir Ethelred de Fortebrand, who is here present."

The Abbot now approached the throne on which Sir Ethelred was seated, and, slowly bending his knee, retired; and, after him, followed the other monks, each paying the same obeisance.

The haughty De Fortebrand scarce deigned to move his head, even when the Abbot bent before him, but surveyed the venerable train with a supercilious regard.

As soon as they had all passed before De Fortebrand, the train left the Castle in the same manner in which they had advanced to it, and returned to the Abbey.

As the day was too far advanced for him to see the Lady Elinor, the Abbot went not; but, in his superb apartments, sat restless and miserable, forming plans in his mind of the most dreadful vengeance on Sir Ethelred, for the severe mortification his pride had undergone.

Father Oswald, who had long resided at De Clifford Castle, called at the Abbey in the evening, and informed the Abbot that he had that day received a letter from De Clifford, who had so long been supposed dead, acquainting him that he was then in Venice, having fortunately escaped from some banditti, in whose strong-holds he had been detained; and that he purposed, as soon as he could obtain a vessel, to proceed to his estate.

Full of this intelligence, the Abbot appeared the next morning before the Lady Elinor, whom he found brooding over the insult she had received from Sir Ethelred, in his denial of her request, and also of his deceit in possessing himself of her domains, with a view to recover his exhausted finances.

She welcomed the Abbot, on his approach, with a smile, and, desiring him to seat himself, immediately entered on the subject nearest her heart, namely, the wrongs she had received from

De Fortebrand; she saw herself in a moment stripped of all her large possessions by a needy adventurer, one too who had acted contrary to her request, and whom she now resolved to deprive of the power of further thwarting her wishes.

The Abbot listened to the recital of her wrongs, and professed himself ready to assist her in any plans she might form to satisfy her vengeance; and, looking at Elinor, with a particular expression in his countenance, said—"And now, Lady, I have a piece of news to make you acquainted with, which will, doubtless, greatly surprise you."

"What is it?" hastily demanded Elinor; "pray inform me, holy Father?"

"It is," rejoined the Abbot, "that Sir Henry De Clifford, whom you so long lamented as dead, still lives."

"Lives!" exclaimed Lady Elinor: "good heavens, is it possible! De Clifford still alive, and I another's! Perish the thought! No; this arm shall first——But tell me, I beseech you, Father," said she, "is it true or is it only a fabrication? How heard you, how did you obtain the intelligence?"

"Yesterday evening, Lady," returned the Abbot, "as I was sitting alone, oppressed with grief, and thinking on the degradation I had experienced in the morning, Father Oswald, who, you know, has long resided at De Clifford Castle, came to see me, and from him I learnt that he had received a letter from De Clifford, who was then at Venice, and who expected soon to sail for Albion's bold shores: this was the manner, Lady, in which I received the information, and which you may depend on as being correct; for, you well know, Father Oswald is too strict, and too pious a man, to advance any thing without a proper foundation."

The Lady Elinor paid the greatest attention to the speech of Bertrand; and, when he had done, sat for a few minutes silent, devising in what manner she could best bring about the dark schemes she was planning.

The Abbot saw how much the knowledge of De Clifford, who she had so much adored, being still in existence had affected her; he saw, too, how favourable it would prove to his desire of vengeance against Sir Ethelred; and, thinking it would be best to leave her to her own meditations, he bowed lowly, gave her his benediction, and retired.

As he was passing through the great hall, he met Sir Ethelred, who was at that moment crossing it; the Abbot made his obeisance, but the haughty De Fortebrand passed on without deigning to notice it.

This conduct served to fix still deeper the deadly shafts of hatred and malice in his heart, and to accelerate his dark designs concerning him.

The Abbot now, slowly winding down the romantic path which led to the valley below, soon found himself at the gates of the Abbey of Ford, where the adulation and respect that was paid him, served but to encrease the resentment he harboured against Sir Ethelred.

From the haughty Lady Elinor de Fortebrand, and her furious and revengeful disposition, he saw a most complete tool for his purposes, which he could make use of against Sir Ethelred; he saw, also, the effect the arrival of De Clifford appeared to have upon her; he heard her sudden exclamation, and broken sentences, and saw that her plots against Sir Ethelred were nearly formed, and trusted she would soon find means to carry them into effect, of whatever nature they were.

END OF VOLUME ONE.

THE

CASTLE

OF

BERRY POMEROY.

A Novel.

⫷⫸

IN TWO VOLUMES.

⫷⫸

BY

EDWARD MONTAGUE,

AUTHOR OF

MONTONI, OR THE CONFESSIONS OF THE MONK OF ST.
BENEDICT, &c.

Nought is there under Heaven's wide hollowness,
That moves more dear compassion of the mind,
Than beauty brought t'unworthy wretchedness,
By Envy's snares, or Fortune's freaks unkind.

SPENSER.

VOL. II.

LONDON:
PRINTED AT THE
Minerva-Press,
FOR LANE, NEWMAN, AND CO.
LEADENHALL-STREET.
1806.

THE
CASTLE OF BERRY POMEROY

CHAPTER I.

"Now o'er the one half world
  Nature seems dead, and wicked dreams abuse
  The curtain'd sleep: now witchcraft celebrates
  Pale Hecate's offerings; and withered murther,
  Alarum'd by his centinel, the wolf,
  Whose howls his watch, thus with his stealthy pace,
  With Tarquin's ravishing strides, tow'rds his design
  Moves like a ghost. Thou sure and firm set earth,
  Hear not my steps, which way they walk, for fear
  Thy very stones prate of my whereabouts."

SHAKESPEARE.

WHEN Elinor was left alone in her apartment, the intelligence brought her by the Abbot left not a vacuum in her mind: the idea of De Clifford returned in all its former strength and fondness.

"Perhaps," thought she, "time and change of scene has obliterated from his mind his grief for Matilda: and now that there is a likelihood, or possibility, that he might pay his addresses to me, I have myself put an entire bar to the completion of my most ardent wish, and given myself to a man who has not only imposed upon me, but also insulted me, and dared to deny what I even sued for:—and, is it possible that Elinor can put up with such injurious treatment? no, no, forbid it, fate! De Fortebrand, thy doom is fixed. Oh that that act would but insure me De Clifford, my soul's far dearest part! with what pleasure would I this instant carry it into execution! but I must be cautious, lest the lowering eye of suspicion glance at me. To-morrow I will commune with the Abbot, who, justly incensed, as well as myself, against Sir Ethelred, will, no doubt, gladly enter into my schemes."

Such were the ruminations of the revengeful Elinor, whose heart, now hardened against the stings of conscience, could tamely deliberate on the taking off of a man, whom she had accepted as her husband, and had sworn at the altar to love and obey.

But an affront was what Elinor could not forgive; and, he had not only been guilty of that, but also had deceived her with respect to his circumstances, in order to obtain her hand; and what now weighed more heavily against him than all, was, that De Clifford, the beloved De Clifford, still existed, to the possession of whom he was an insurmountable obstacle.

Early the next morning, she dispatched a messenger to Ford, to request the Abbot would see her that day, which he promised to do, and the agitated Elinor awaited his arrival with impatience.

When he entered the chamber, "Father," said she, "Fortebrand's doom is fixed."

"Be it so, Lady," said the pleased Abbot: "in what manner, fair daughter, dost thou propose to accomplish the deed?"

"Of that I would commune with thee, Father: our actions must be so dark, so well contrived, as not to leave room for suspicion.—Sir Ethelred goes hence to-morrow, to his castle on the banks of the winding Dart, and returns not till the shades of the evening descend: would not that afford an opportunity, Father, of putting our wishes into execution?"

"In what manner, Lady?" replied the Abbot. "Who wouldst though employ?"

"Thyself, Father—who else can I confide in."

"Me, Lady!" said the Abbot—"how?—'tis impossible."

"Father," said Elinor, perceiving his irresolution, rising up from her seat, and opening a large coffer which was in the apartment, "do that, and this is thy reward," presenting him with a large packet, on which was inscribed, "The title of Sir Hugh De Pomeroy to the Abbey of Ford and its lands."

Quickly did the Abbot glance his delighted eyes over this superscription. "Lady," said he, "I will accomplish the deed; but think not I am the more instigated to serve you, from this your generous bounty; no, Lady, my poor endeavours to contribute to your happiness shall ever be exerted in your behalf."

So spake the Abbot; and Elinor, who knew his rapacity too well, to think what he said true, affected to believe him, and even thanked him for his disinterested friendship.

"Daughter," said he, "in two days you will again see me, when, perhaps, he who has so greatly injured you will receive the due reward of his crimes."

So saying, putting the writings beneath his garments, he retired from the presence of the Lady Elinor, with evident satisfaction, for he had at length obtained what he had so much longed, so much wished for.

He now revolved in his mind how he was to perpetrate the deed, without fear of detection: to attack De Fortebrand would be little short of madness, as he might himself fall in the dark attempt. A thought now struck him, as appearing to be the easiest and safest way of effecting it. When at the Castle of Sir Henry Fitz-Auburne, he had much accustomed himself to the use of the bow, and had become an expert archer.

He therefore determined to endeavour to wound De Fortebrand, as he was passing on his return to the Castle, through a small wood, whose impending branches so darkened the place, that he might advance near the spot where his victim must pass, and thus ensure himself success in his dark project.

One difficulty only remained, and that was, how to procure the instruments of death: however, it at length occurred to him, that as he must that night visit the Castle of Berry Pomeroy, for some reasons known only to himself, he could perhaps, in the dead silence of night, penetrate into the armoury of the Castle, where he could easily procure a bow and arrows.

He had now reached the Abbey, and proceeded immediately to his chamber, anxious to peruse the papers relative to the lands attached to the Abbey of Ford, which now belonged to him.

Thus passed the evening, and when the dark-robed curtain of night was drawn over the face of nature, he left the Abbey, by a private postern, and proceeded, through the well-known path, to the Castle of Berry Pomeroy.

Into this edifice he could at all times gain access, by a small door which was sunk in the earth, and covered with over-hanging bushes, which, when thrust aside, disclosed a few steps that led down to the portal, of which he had for a long time kept the key: this opened into the subterraneous passages which were under the Castle, and had a communication with the chapel, which was near the great hall, and through which he could enter the armoury.

Whatever Bertrand's business was at the Castle, it was apparent that it was of a secret nature, by the care he took to conceal his person, which on such occasions he muffled up in a large mantle, which entirely covered his face, and the form of his body; and the dark hour of midnight, that he chose for such visitation, proved that it was of great import.

The Abbot, crossing these subterraneous passages, ascended some stone steps which led into the Castle chapel, and then cautiously pacing the grand aisle, opened the folding doors, and proceeded through the hall, and then entered a long corridor, which communicated with the several apartments on that side of the Castle: with caution he opened the door of the armoury, and selected, by the light of his lamp, a bow and some arrows, from among the numerous heaps that were scattered about.

Having thus attained what he wanted, he returned the same way he had come, through the chapel, and taking up a basket which he had brought with him, and which he had left in the chapel, he descended the steps, and crossing the vaults in an opposite direction to the way he had before traced, came to a small apartment, which he entered, and lifting up a trap-door in one corner of it, lowered the basket by a rope, into the place below; then carefully closing the trap-door, and fastening the door of the apartment, he retraced his steps, and crossing the subterraneous vaults, emerged from their damp recesses, at the hidden door under the walls of the Castle: this he carefully locked, and with the bow and arrows he had taken from the armoury, directed his steps to Ford Abbey, which he entered at a private gate, which communicated by a passage to his apartments, and by means of which, he could at any time leave the Abbey unperceived, and effect his purposes abroad, while he was supposed to be engaged in his own oratory, in the solemn exercises of devotion and religious meditations; but how widely-different were past the ill-spent hours of the dark-plotting, revengeful, and avaricious Bertrand!

Meanwhile the Lady Elinor calmed the agitations of her mind, by reflecting that the Abbot would soon do away the origin of them; and in order that she might not be suspected as the contriver of the death of Sir Ethelred, she on the same day that Bertrand had been with her, signified to her domestics that she should dine with him in the hall. This act, she thought, would serve as a token that she had forgiven the conduct of Sir Ethelred towards her.

De Fortebrand, on consideration, was sorry that he had so haughtily demeaned himself to the Lady Elinor, and which he would not perhaps have done, had he not been so greatly incensed at the conduct of the Abbot; for he well knew that it was much his interest to endeavour to gain her affections, as the severe disappointment she must soon come to the knowledge of, concerning the state of his affairs, would otherwise tend to widen the breach already made, beyond all possibility of reparation.

When, therefore, he learnt that she intended that day to dine in his company, he understood it, as Elinor wished he should, to be a step made by her towards a reconciliation, and was, for the reasons above mentioned, much pleased with the circumstance.

When, therefore, he saw her descend the grand staircase, he advanced to meet her, and taking her hand, placed her at the table, and during the repast, entered into the frequent conversation with her, and which the Lady Elinor apparently attended to with pleasure.

The numerous domestics, who knew of the great disagreement that had been between them, surveyed the sudden change with some astonishment, and which they were unable to account for.

As soon as the repast was ended, Sir Ethelred poured some wine in a goblet, which he presented to the Lady Elinor, who gracefully received it from his hand, and partook of the contents;—and then, rising up, was conducted by Sir Ethelred to the portal of the hall, which opened on the staircase, where, bowing low, he left her attended by her women, who were in waiting.

Thus did they mutually endeavour to deceive, the easier to conceal the dark plans each were plotting against the other. De Fortebrand, that he might more easily appropriate to his own use and purposes, her extensive possessions; and the Lady Elinor, that she might, without suspicion, rid herself of a man against whom she bore the most irreconcilable hatred, and whose destruction she had determined on.

CHAPTER II.

"Come, thick night,
And pall thee in the dunnest smoke of hell,
That my keen dart see not the wound it makes;
Nor heaven peep through the blanket of the dark,
To cry hold! hold!"

SHAKESPEARE.

"Oh! I am shot; a forked burning arrow
Sticks in my side; the sad venom flies
Like lightning through my flesh, my blood, my marrow:
Ha! what a change of torments I endure!
A bolt of ice runs hissing through my body:
'Tis sure the arm of death."

LEE.

WHEN the evening approached in dusky array, the Abbot Bertrand disguised himself in a peasant's habit, and with the bow and arrows he had taken from the armoury of the Castle of Berry Pomeroy, whose points he had previously dipped in the juice of deadly herbs, sallied from the private postern, and gained the wood through which he knew De Fortebrand must pass in his way from his own mansion to Berry Pomeroy Castle.

He took his station by the side of the road, concealed by a clump of knotty oaks, and seating himself on their emerging roots, waited with anxious expectancy, until the echo of horses' hoofs should break on the silence around, and foretell the approach of De Fortebrand.

The shades of night began to thicken, and the wind howled amongst the leafy tenants of the forest, when Bertrand heard the approaching paces of a steed; instantly he prepared to execute his dire intent—soon the horseman drew near, and, recognizing in him the haughty De Fortebrand, Bertrand drew his arrow to its barbed point and buried it deep in his side.

Sir Ethelred, uttering a deep groan, clapped his spurs to his horse, and was soon out of sight. Bertrand instantly quitted the place, and cautiously retraced his steps to the Abbey; having first cast away into the waves of the winding Dart, the bow and arrows that remained.

Sir Ethelred continued his rapid course, with the arrow deep planted in his side; at length, overcome with the pain, and loss of blood, he dropped from his horse, and lay extended, and almost inanimate, on the ground.

The horse stopped not till he came to the drawbridge of Berry Pomeroy Castle, when the warden, who was in expectation of the arrival of Sir Ethelred, advanced to meet him; but, when he saw the steed without his rider, he instantly conceived that his Lord had been thrown, and immediately repaired to the Lady Elinor, to make her acquainted with the circumstance.

"Lady," said he, "the steed of Sir Ethelred is arrived, but without our Lord; and much my mind misgives me, that some accident has happened him: will it please you, Lady, to direct a party to search the woods, for perhaps should he have been thrown, he may need assistance?"

"The saints forefend!" wildly exclaimed Elinor. "Run, good warden; delay not, I entreat you, to rescue my beloved Lord; myself will follow too."

"Nay, Lady," said the warden, "the night is dark and bleak; ill it would agree with thy gentle form: Lady, be assured of our faithful services—I will away anon."

"The saints speed and guide you!" returned the Lady Elinor; and apparently overcome with the emotions and agitation of her mind, sunk, seemingly devoid of life, on a couch.

The warden, summoning a party of domestics, left the Castle to seek Sir Ethelred; they took the road that led to his mansion, on the green banks of the Dart, where they knew he had directed his course in the morning; and at length discovered him, laying on the ground, with the fatal arrow in his side.

The warden hastily drew the arrow, and examined the body,

to find if the vital spark was quite extinguished; but Sir Ethelred had departed his mortal tenement, and was now summoned to render up an account of the evil deeds of his life.

Hastily pulling down some of the branches of the surrounding trees, the servants formed a sort of bier, on which they laid the breathless form; and with slow steps proceeded towards the Castle.

When they had deposited the body in the hall, the Lady Elinor was made acquainted with the fatal circumstance.

Frantic with grief, and uttering exclamations of distress, she wildly rushed into the hall, and sunk insensible by the side of Sir Ethelred. The female domestics instantly conveyed her to her apartments; and the warden sent a messenger to the Abbot, to make him acquainted with what had happened to Sir Ethelred.

Bertrand, when he arrived at the private postern, proceeded instantly to his chamber, where he immediately, casting aside his disguise, threw himself on his pallet, in order that when he should be sent for, he might be thus found.

According to his expectation, he some hours after heard a loud knocking at the gate of the Abbey, and soon after the voice of one of the monks at the door of his chamber, calling to him.

"Enter, my son," said he; "what weighty affair is it that brings thee here, at the silent hour of midnight?"

"Father," said the monk, "a breathless messenger from the Lady Elinor De Fortebrand instantly requests your attendance at the Castle. The man reports his Lord to have been but a few hours ago found in the forest, slain by a barbed arrow, that was deep rooted in his side."

"The saints preserve us!" exclaimed the Abbot, rising up: "let the messenger attend me here, while I prepare myself to go to the Castle, that I may question him about this dolorous event."

The monk departed, and soon returned with the man, who related what he had already told the monk; and as soon as the Abbot was ready, preceded him with a torch.

When he arrived at the Castle, and had entered the hall, the first object that presented itself to his eyes was the murdered body of Sir Ethelred De Fortebrand, laying on a table.

Unprepared for the sight, the Abbot started back, with horror in his countenance; his trembling limbs refused their office; and, but for a domestic, who, seeing his agitation, supported him, he would have fallen to the ground. For some moments he could not keep his eyes from gazing on the corpse. At length, with the greatest difficulty, he in some degree composed the internal agitation of his mind; and proceeded slowly along the hall, with downcast eyes and trembling steps.

By the time, however, that he reached the apartments of the Lady Elinor, he had recovered himself: he found her laying on her couch, with her face covered, and her female attendants standing round her.

When the Abbot entered the chamber, she motioned to the attendants to withdraw; and as soon as the room was cleared, she gazed on the Abbot:

"Did you see him?" said she, in a low voice. "Oh God! how horrible he looked!"

"Name it not, Lady," said Bertrand; "I am as yet but scarcely recovered from the agitation the sight threw me in. But, Lady, this is no moment for conversation of such a nature as this; compose your spirits—I will endeavour to calm my agitations also. But, tell me, are there any suspicious hints thrown out, about the way of his death?"

"My domestics have told me," returned Elinor, "that the arrow which was found in his body, from the appearance of the wound caused by it, must have been poisoned—say, Father, was it so?"

" 'Tis true, Lady, it was so," returned the Abbot; "I did it for the greater security. Our plans have succeeded, and now you may again entertain hopes of possessing the amiable De Clifford."

This idea afforded comfort to the frame of the Lady Elinor, and for some moments she was silent, indulging a reverie on that hapless being, with whose manly beauties she was so fascinated.

At length she again addressed the Abbot—"Father," said

she, "your longer stay here may create suspicion: you know there are requisite attentions to be paid to the departed Sir Ethelred; endeavour to compose yourself sufficiently to see these performed."

Shuddering at again being obliged to view the blood-stained corpse, the Abbot slowly withdrew from the chamber, and ordering the females to attend on their lady, he proceeded to the hall.

The body was then conveyed to an apartment, where the Abbot performed the ceremonies prescribed by the Romish Church; and having appointed the time for the interment to be on the evening of the third day, he departed from the Castle, lit on his way by the rising splendour of the morning sun.

The domestics of Berry Pomeroy Castle all agreed in one point, namely, that their late Lord had been murdered; the circumstance of the arrow being poisoned, confirming that idea. The warden too, on examining the arrow, found, by a certain mark on it, that it had belonged to the Castle armoury: this then made it appear that it must have been some person belonging to the Castle that had perpetrated the deed: and not knowing any one on whom to fix their suspicions, mutually suspected each other; and each regarded his fellow with a look of distrust.

Not the least breath of suspicion, however, attached itself to the Lady Elinor or the Abbot; and time was looked forward to, as being only able to unravel the mystery.

Preparations were now made at the Castle for the interment of Sir Ethelred:—the walls of the great hall, and of the chamber in which he lay, were hung with mournful black; the Castle chapel was also habited in like manner; and a respectful silence reigned under the lofty roofs of Berry Pomeroy Castle, while the body of its lord remained uninterred.

Thus fell Sir Ethelred De Fortebrand, by the arts and contrivances of the Lady Elinor, whom he had played so foul and a deadly a game to possess, in the taking off of Sir Hugh De Seymour; and had beside used mean dissimulation in his expressions of fondness for her, since it was only for her vast possessions for which he sighed, and which had spurred him on to commit so horrible a crime, as that of the destruction of a fellow-creature, a circumstance that in after ages produced civil discord and contentions; for some mariners, who were below the cliff in a boat, endeavouring to ensnare the finny race, saw the deed which Sir Ethelred performed, in thrusting the unwary De Seymour off the lofty cliff; they observed him too after that, slowly winding among the rocks which lead to the shores of the Dart.

These circumstances were not related to any one, as the vessel to which they belonged, impelled by a favouring breeze, soon after sailed; but coming to the port some years after, and hearing of the circumstances we have here related, immediately repeated what they had seen; and the time and place agreeing, it began to be suspected that it must have been De Fortebrand who was the cause of Sir Hugh De Seymour's death: and the circumstance of their having at the same time paid their addresses to an heiress of the Castle of Berry Pomeroy, whom De Fortebrand afterwards married, confirmed the idea, and in after ages produced war and bloodshed; for the De Seymours, in revenge, attacked the Castle of Berry Pomeroy, and at last succeeded in taking it, and in their possession it has since remained; but the unjust spirits who inhabited its lofty walls, rendered it impossible for them to reside in it; and time at length has reduced it to the romantic ruins, which are to this day to be seen near the ancient town of Totness.

CHAPTER III.

"Methought, even now, I mark'd the starts of guilt
That shook her soul; though damn'd dissimulation
Skreen'd her dark thoughts, and set to public view
A specious face of innocence and beauty:
Oh false appearance!—"

ROWE.

TOWARDS the close of the evening of the day appointed for the interment of Sir Ethelred de Fortebrand, the Abbot entered the hall, with a long train of monks and choristers.

The coffin, in which was the pale remains of De Fortebrand, was borne by his domestics, from the chamber where it had lain, and placed in the centre of the hall; and the domestics, with torches in their hands, were ranged around it. As the Abbot entered, the choristers chaunted a solemn hymn; and the servants bearing the body of Sir Ethelred, the procession ranging themselves in order, proceeded to the Castle chapel.

First slowly walked six domestics, with torches; then appeared a monk, bearing a crucifix; then followed another, holding on a velvet cushion a missal, both bare-headed; next came the Abbot, with a monk on each side; next followed the body, borne by eight of the domestics; after that were pages, bearing his banner, reversed, and his helmet, sword and shield; next came the castellain, habited in deep mourning; after him the wardens, and other officers of the household; then came a long train of the fathers, habited in their flowing garments; and after them followed the choristers, and the remainder of the domestics, bearing torches.

In this manner they proceeded into the chapel, where the coffin was set down on a marble table, before the altar, when the Abbot, taking the missal from the monk who bore it, with a faltering voice began to read the first part of the service of the dead.

This concluded, the men then bearing the coffin, proceeded in the same form, down to the vaults below, where the cold form of Sir Ethelred was committed to the grave.

The torches which the domestics held, but faintly illumined the dusky recesses of these abodes of death, and those places where the light could not penetrate were lost in shapeless misty vapours, and encreased the solemnity of the scene.

A slow and deep-toned dirge was now chaunted over the grave, after which the Abbot concluded the service: the vaults now echoed to the sound of the earth, as it rattled on the coffin; and soon the grave was filled up, and the train departed.

The next morning the Abbot came to the Castle, and proceeded to the Lady Elinor, whose smiling countenance, when she was in private converse with him, ill agreed with the sable robes that enveloped her form.

The Abbot now counselled her to set on foot a most minute search after the perpetrators of the murder of Sir Ethelred, which would divert the eye of suspicion, that might otherwise rest on them.

This was accordingly done—parties were continually sent out, and large rewards offered; but, as the reader will easily perceive, to no purpose.

The Lady Elinor rejoiced with the Abbot at the success of their well-constructed plans: and Bertrand, in the possession of the domains of Ford Abbey, buried in oblivion the means by which he had acquired them.

Thus passed on some weeks, and at length the Abbot came one morning to the Castle, before his usual time: "Lady," said he, to Elinor, "I have news of a joyful import for your ear."

"What is it, Father?" said she; "is it ought concerning Sir Henry De Clifford? is he arrived?"

"He is, fair daughter," replied the Abbot. "This morning the vessel which bore him from the Venetian shores, anchored in the bay, and he is now proceeding to his Castle, amidst the acclamations of his delighted domestics."

"The saints be praised for it," said the Lady Elinor. "Oh Father, how my heart beats with indescribable emotions! Think you, Father, he will ever come under the shelter of these roofs?—shall I ever again behold him?"

"Doubtless," replied the Abbot, "he will now no longer remain insensible to the charms of the Lady Elinor, and will soon become a suitor to the fair inhabitant of Berry Pomeroy Castle."

"Well, Father," said the sighing Elinor, "a short time will now discover the foundation on which my hopes of happiness are built."

What was Elinor's delight to hear, on the next morning, that a domestic was arrived from De Clifford, bearing a message of condolement for her late loss. Not satisfied with sending an answer, the Lady Elinor bade the messenger wait, and she would herself give him audience; and descending into the hall, saw Hubert, a faithful domestic of De Clifford's, which assured her he took no common interest in the message, having dispatched it by his own favourite attendant.

The Lady Elinor having learnt from Hubert the words of his master, and returned a suitable reply, she desired the chief warden of the Castle would make welcome to it the domestic of Sir Henry De Clifford; and with a light heart returned to her apartments.

The Abbot, to whom she next day related the circumstance, augured favourably of it, and gave her joy on the seeming approaching fulfillment of her wishes.

Some days now passed, and the Lady Elinor anxiously awaited that happy one which would bring De Clifford to see her; for she conceived that if he had had no intention of cultivating her acquaintance, he would not have sent his servant to the Castle, with so friendly a message to her.

One evening as she was retiring to her couch, she heard the long blast of a horn at the Castle gates; and soon after several of the domestics came to the door of her apartment, and informed her that the Castle was beset by soldiery.

The Lady Elinor now opened the door, and saw, by the pallid looks of the attendants, how much the circumstance alarmed them. The castellain now hastily approached.

"Lady," said he, "a numerous band of soldiery are arrived, in front of the Castle, and claim admittance, in the name of the King."

"The saints defend us!" exclaimed the affrighted Elinor, "what can they want? Attend me," said she, to the castellain, "to the tower that overhangs the bridge; and immediately give orders that the portcullis be lowered. I will know their business, ere they enter the lofty towers of Berry Pomeroy Castle: meanwhile, let all my domestics arm themselves, in case the bridge should be attacked."

Elinor now ascending into one of the turret chambers that flanked the gate, commanded the warden to sound his horn, which being instantly returned, she opened the casement, and, to her fear-struck eyes, appeared a numerous band of soldiers.

Endeavouring to conceal her agitation, "Who is it," said she, addressing herself to the officer that commanded, "that thus disturbs the repose of my Castle, at this solitary hour?"

"Our orders, Lady," said the commander, "must plead our excuse; we bear the King's mandate, which may not be disobeyed; and sorry am I to say, it is directed against thee, Lady, if thou art the Lady Elinor de Fortebrand."

"Against me!" said the affrighted Elinor: "with what crime am I charged, that should urge the hand of sovereign power against me?"

"Of that, Lady, I am ignorant," replied the officer; "my instructions relate only to the detention of your person; and sorry am I that the lot, to execute such an unpleasant duty, has fallen on me."

"Nay then," said the Lady Elinor, "it is not fitting that I should admit into my Castle so numerous a troop, without full convincement of your just intentions; if, as you say, ye bear a mandate against me, ye must surely know why such is issued;

and, until I have better authority for so doing, the bridge of Berry Pomeroy Castle descends not."

"Then, Lady," returned the officer, "my instructions are to force the Castle; therefore I pray you, Lady, spare the needless effusion of blood, in a resistance of no import to the brave men I lead, and deliver up thyself to the King's authority."

"Thy words are useless, to persuade me to so rash an act," returned the Lady Elinor. "If thy intents were just, the sun would have beheld thy forces at my gate, and thou wouldst not thus, under cover of the gloom of night, seek, by thy feigned story, admission within my walls: therefore, if longer you here remain, my archers will have orders to direct their winged messengers of death against you."

"Be heedful, Lady," returned the officer, "how you despise and contemn the authority that sent me here, and which will heavily revert on yourself, and become a crime of a nature difficult to be excused."

The officer then beckoned to an inferior, who was near him, awaiting his orders, and having conversed a few moments with him; the man, making his military salute, retired, and soon disappeared in the thick surrounding gloom.

Elinor, who saw this circumstance, and began to be fearful that they would attempt to force the Castle, now thought it her safest plan to endeavour to gain some time, during which she might make her escape, for she began to have a thousand fears take root in her mind, and which encreased every moment.

She therefore thus addressed the officer: "If," said she, "the commission ye are charged with the execution of, is of the nature ye aver, withdraw your forces for the night, and to-morrow's dawn ye shall have free admission."

"Nay, Lady," returned the officer, "it must not be so, nor will I remove my troops till my orders are obeyed; therefore, Lady, longer parley is needless; and my duty to my sovereign will quickly oblige me to use harsh means."

Elinor knew not what steps to take; she was well convinced

that the small number of her domestics could not long withstand the vigorous attack of men expert in the art of warfare; nor could the castellain, to whom she applied, direct her what course to follow. In this dilemma she remained for some time, and looking from her casement, beheld the troops busied in surrounding the Castle.

A confused noise soon after met her ear, and she then heard several voices exclaiming, "the Castle is seized;" and a croud of the domestics rushed affrighted into the chamber, followed by a party of soldiers, who had entered the Castle by the subterraneous vaults, the leader of whom ordered her, in the King's name, to surrender.

The Lady Elinor, convinced that now all resistance was useless, quietly submitted; and passing down the turret stairs, commanded the portcullis to be drawn up, and the bridge lowered.

The commanding officer now advanced, and respectfully making his obeisance, conducted her to a covered car, into which she ascended, and, escorted by a party of soldiery, was conveyed to a place of confinement, on the opposite side of the Dart, where the officer left her in strict charge of the wardens of the place.

CHAPTER IV.

> "Ambition is at distance
> A goodly prospect, tempting to the view;
> The height delights us; and the mountain-top
> Looks beautiful, because 'tis nigh to heaven:
> But we ne'er think how sandy's the foundation,
> What storms will batter, and what tempests shake us."
>
> OTWAY.

THE officer having thus safely placed the Lady Elinor De Fortebrand, called off his forces from the Castle of Berry Pomeroy; for he had no orders respecting the keeping it in possession, but was to leave it to the care of the castellain, till a new claimant should arrive. He then pursued the winding path that led through the vale beneath, towards the Abbey of Ford. The bright beams of the morning sun now glittered on the arms of the soldiers, and their battle spears reflected its dazzling refulgence.

The Abbot returned from his last interview with the Lady Elinor, pleased with having so successfully accomplished all his plans, without even drawing on himself the eye of suspicion. The deeds that forced him to fly the Castle of Fitz-Auburne, were now, he trusted, buried in oblivion; nor did he think that it could be possible to recognize the humble Walter, in the Abbot of Ford: he was now fatigued with paying such servile court to the Lady Elinor; and looked forward with some hopes, now that De Clifford seemed inclined to renew the short acquaintance he had had with her, that he would pay his much-desired addresses to her, and then he well knew his attentions would not be missed, and he should be able to enjoy more entirely the splendor and luxuries arising from his situation; and now too that the extensive domains of the Abbey belonged to him, he had more means of gratifying his desires.

From the Lady Elinor he had no more to expect, and his visits to her now grew tedious; he was no more dependent on her; and the link of iniquity was the only one that connected them; but that was strong, because their interest and their personal safety rendered it necessary it should be so.

The next morning, as the Abbot was employed in ruminating on the great success that had attended him, word was brought that a band of armed men were approaching towards the Abbey, by the grand avenue.

Surprised at so unusual a circumstance, the Abbot arose, and entering on a long open gallery, which ran over the portico in front of the building, viewed the party as they approached.

From their regular and well-appointed appearance, he was well convinced that they were the King's forces, and was involved in a maze of doubt and conjecture as to the motive of their visit;

and he awaited in anxious suspense, till they should arrive. At length the officer riding up to the gates of the Abbey, demanded permission to speak with Father Bertrand, the Abbot.

The porter of the Abbey having delivered this message to Bertrand, who, on the approach of the officer, had retired from the balcony, now again advanced to it, and leaning over the balustrades, thus spoke to the commander:—

"What wouldst thou, my son, with the Abbot? Behold him before you—speak your purpose, and why those men, in arms, attend thee, with seeming hostile intents?"

"Holy Father," said the officer, looking up to the Abbot, "the message I am charged with is of no pleasant import: the King, my master, hath issued his mandate, which I bear, for the safe-keeping of thy person, until his further royal will and pleasure be known."

"And how is that to be effected?" haughtily replied the Abbot, though inwardly trembling with undescribable emotions: "know ye not that these walls may not be polluted by your entrance? I here attend the wishes of the King, thy master, but I acknowledge no other supreme power than the Pope, nor will I bend to other controul: thou mayst then, my son, bear this answer back, for thy present errand is fruitless: how couldst thou suppose, or bear in thy mind one instant, that the members of the holy church would ever submit to laical jurisdiction? His holiness the Pope's legate is now on England's shores; depart then to him, and what he will, I in duty am bound to obey."

The Abbot then haughtily retired, disdaining further converse; he had hoped that the officer would, on hearing the latter part of his speech, withdraw his troops, and give him an opportunity of escape.

But this the commander, unfortunately for him, thought might be the case; and seeing that it was not possible for him to enter the Abbey, and take the Abbot by force, since he well knew he was not warranted in performing such an act, but had hoped to have surprised the Abbot, and having once got him from the sanctuary of the Abbey walls, would not have hesitated to conduct him, according to his orders.

Seeing, however, that he was foiled in his attempts, he instantly dispatched a horseman to the King's court, to relate the impediments to his performing that part of his orders which related to the Abbot, and what he had done with respect to the Lady Elinor; and determined that the Abbot should not, in the interval of the messenger's absence, escape, he posted centinels round the walls of the Abbey; and ordered the men to pitch their tents, and await the return of the courier.

Meanwhile the Abbot's mind was filled with distracting fears and apprehensions; he was ignorant of what particular crime he was charged with; and of all the diabolical acts of his life, he knew but one that could bring on him the vengeful arm of justice; but the more he considered it, the more he felt assured of its impossibility; and should he be longer kept confined in the Abbey walls, he knew that channel to a discovery would soon be no more.

To attempt to escape was impossible, as the soldiers guarded with the utmost vigilance every entrance to the Abbey; even the peasantry who supplied it with provisions, were not allowed to enter the walls, but were obliged to deposit their burthens before the gate, from whence the lay brethren were allowed to come out to bring them in.

He therefore had only to hope that his usual good fortune would not desert him, and that he should yet be able to make his escape; and awaited the further proceedings of the party, with some outward appearance of composure.

The messenger, sent by the officer, travelled with the utmost speed, and soon arrived at the court, where he delivered his dispatches.

The Pope's legate happened to be there at the same time, and therefore the subject of his message was the sooner arranged, and a sealed packet committed to his care, to be delivered to the officer, on his arrival, for his further directions.

As soon as the man arrived, he delivered the packet he was charged with to the officer, who, breaking the seals, found a roll of paper addressed to Father Oswald, and a direction to him, to cause the same to be conveyed to the Father, at De Clifford Castle.

Wondering at what this could mean, he instantly obeyed the orders: and on the messenger's return, learnt that the Father would be with him early the next morning.

Accordingly the venerable Father Oswald, soon after the rays of the sun had dispelled the misty vapours of the night, appeared before the tent of the officer.

"My son," said he, "the packet you yesterday sent me, contains the following directions. I am ordered to take on me the situation of Abbot of Ford, in the place of the present superior, Father Bertrand. The Pope's legate desires me to acquaint you, that you are not to detain the Father, who, having borne the high office of Abbot is not to be subject to laical authority, but that he is to be confined in the Abbey, until he shall be exonerated of certain acts that he hath been accused of; and you are to remain here until he is in safe custody, and to lend your aid, should it be found necessary, to enforce obedience to the commands of the holy legate."

"I obey with all humility, reverend Father," replied the officer, "to whatever may be thought most fitting to be done by the Pope's legate, and you too, holy Father."

"I must now," said Oswald, "convene the Fathers in the hall, when I shall explain to them my orders, and shew my authority; and in case your assistance should be found necessary, I shall cause a signal to be made to you." The officer respectfully bowed, and the Father proceeded towards the Abbey gates.

Having called together the religious community, and Father Bertrand, he read to them the letters he had received.

The good Fathers, who all respected Father Oswald, were rejoiced at the change that was now taking place, and hailed their new superior with acclamations of delight.

Bertrand stood aghast and confounded, nor dared to lift up his eyes, lest they should meet the reproachful looks of those over whom he had lately presided, with so tyrannical a sway.

Father Oswald being now acknowledged Abbot of Ford, directed that the order of the Pope's legate should be carried into effect, and that Father Bertrand be stripped of his rich habiliments as Abbot; and that he be taken to one of the cells, appointed to confine criminals in, until the further pleasure of the legate should be known.

Bertrand disdained to make resistance; and silently threw aside the habit he wore, and put on that of a monk; he was then conducted by the lay brethren, to the solitary dungeon of the Abbey; and one of the lay brothers ordered to attend him with provisions.

Thus were the Lady Elinor De Fortebrand and her dark accomplice, Father Bertrand, at last in the power of the strong arm of justice. To account for these extraordinary circumstances, the history must go back to that period when De Clifford, oppressed with grief for the loss of his adored Matilda, determined to leave his native shores, and, by a change of scene and clime, endeavour to drive away the clouds of sorrow which hung over his weak form.

The singular misfortunes he was doomed to meet with in his travels, shall be the subject of the following pages: these, however, he bore with a pious resignation; and, placing his reliance in that Providence, who never deserts his creatures, who look up to him as the anchor they place their trust and confidence in, finally surmounted; and revisited, as the reader is already made acquainted with, the happy shores of England.

CHAPTER V.

The Adventures of De Clifford.

"In his black thoughts, revenge and slaughter roll;
And scenes of blood rise dreadful in his soul."

POPE.

"My mind, and its intents, are savage wild;
More fierce and more inexorable far,
Than empty tigers, or the roaring sea."

SHAKESPEARE.

WHEN De Clifford left his Castle, he journeyed on towards the sea-coast, attended only by a faithful old domestic, named Hubert.

He directed his steps to the sea-coast, and having procured a vessel, embarked for the distant shores of Italy, where he fondly hoped to dissipate his grief, in viewing the wonders of that romantic country.

Prosperous gales winged them swiftly on their way; and in less than three weeks, De Clifford saw the vessel glide by the famous rock, now called Gibraltar, then in possession of the Moors, who at this period were settled in the hilly provinces of Grenada and Andalusia.

Losing sight of the rock, the vessel continued to skim through the liquid plains; and they were now about a week's sail from the Venetian shores, whither they were bound, when, one evening, the master of the vessel descried an Italian brigantine, bearing down upon them.

Supposing that the vessel might be in want of some assistance, the master ordered his bark to lie to, and await their approach.

The brigantine quickly advanced; and coming along-side the vessel, the commander ordered them instantly to surrender, or be cut to pieces.

The master now, too late, found out his mistake, and that he had unfortunately met a pirate. De Clifford, roused from his lethargy, exhorted the men to defend the vessel; and immediately drawing his sword, fell on the party, who were already boarding it, and the crew, animated by his bravery, followed his example.

All was now become a scene of horror and carnage; the deck was strewed with the dead and wounded; De Clifford, assisted by the small crew, twice drove the enemy back to the brigantine, and twice did they return: he now, once more, made them retreat into their own vessel, and followed them: here, however, they made a desperate stand. The commander of the brigantine, seeing the havoc made by De Clifford among his men, rushed on him, and was on the point of running him through the body, when De Clifford quickly turned aside, and avoided the blow, at the same instant wounding the chief in the arm, which was uplifted to destroy him, and forced him to draw back: at this moment, a blow on the head of De Clifford, from one of the banditti behind, caused his senses to forsake him, and he fell, almost lifeless, on the deck.

The crew of the vessel in which De Clifford had sailed, seeing the fate of their leader, for so they styled him, now surrendered themselves to the mercy of their conquerors, who immediately plundered the vessel of the merchandize it contained, and other valuable articles, and then left it to the vanquished crew.

Hubert, who had been desperately wounded in the engagement, saw the fate of his master, and concluded that he was killed: when, therefore, the vessel returned home, he immediately related the sad tale to the sorrowful domestics.

The commander of the brigantine now ordered the bodies of the slain to be cast into the sea; but when they came to De Clifford's, they found him still breathing, and immediately related this circumstance to their leader, whose name was Sebastiano.

A malignant satisfaction gleamed in his dark expressive countenance, and he immediately directed that he should be taken care of, that he might have an opportunity of sating his revenge, for the wound he had received from him, and for the loss of so many of his men.

One of his people, who had formerly studied surgery, was ordered to examine his wound, which he found to be of small consequence, and applying some remedies to it, De Clifford began to revive.

When he opened his eyes, he found himself surrounded by a band of fierce-looking armed men; he seemed, for a short time, to be unconscious of his situation, and his looks wandered about, as if insensible to the objects they gazed on.

Sebastiano, however, did not let him long remain in uncertainty as to his situation, for, advancing to him, "Vile slave," said he, "I will now teach you what it is to contend against me: know, thou art now in my power, and, for thy daring conduct, shall pine away thy tortured existence in the gloomy dungeons of Strombolo."

He directed his men to confine the arms of the unfortunate De Clifford, who, turning to him with a look of disdain, said, "thinkest thou I care for thy threats? no; wert thou a man, thou wouldst not treat me thus: to insult me, now that I cannot revenge it, is the act of a weak boy, and shews the baseness of thy mind:" so saying he turned away, and followed the men into the hold of the vessel, where they secured his legs, and there left him.

Sebastiano now ordered the man at the helm to steer his course for Strombolo, the name of a strong fortress he had on a solitary part of the Italian coast, erected in the bosom of stupendous rocks, and defended by their steep sides.

Towards the close of the second day, the brigantine cast her anchors, at a short distance from an immense ridge of rocks, amongst whose dark recesses rose the Castello De Strombolo, the abode of Sebastiano, who, in its deep caverns, concealed his immense piles of ill-got treasure, and where the rest of his numerous banditti resided.

One of the crew now loosened the cords that confined the limbs of De Clifford, and directed him to follow him to the deck, where, when he arrived, he saw the boat along-side, and Sebastiano in it, who, calling out to his men, ordered them to throw the prisoner into it.

The second in command had, during the engagement, beheld the brave deportment of De Clifford; and, though leagued with Sebastiano, and his banditti, was a brave man, and reverenced that virtue in others. He saw, with the greatest contempt, the behavior of Sebastiano to his unfortunate prisoner; and secretly resolved to alleviate, as much as possible, the horrors of the confinement, which, he well knew, Sebastiano intended to make him endure.

Approaching De Clifford, he told him the orders of his commander; and in a mild tone, requested he would descend the vessel's side, and enter the boat, which was to convey him to Strombolo.

De Clifford, who, till now, had not noticed this man, on looking at him, beheld features of a mild, benevolent, and intelligent cast, unlike the grim and horrible countenance of the fierce Sebastiano: it afforded some comfort to his despairing mind, that there was at least one creature, who bore some affinity to a human being, amongst the numerous sanguinary wretches in whose power he was: he directly complied with the desires of Antoni, for so the second in command was called, and descended into the boat.

The men immediately rowed towards the rocks, and, when close to them, proceeded under the impending cliffs for some time: they then turned into a narrow passage, which scarcely allowed room for the oars to work; by degrees, however, it became larger—and now they were for a time involved in utter darkness, when some gleams of light appeared at a distance, and seemed to shew the extent of the gloomy caverns they were passing through.

A large iron gate now stopped their progress, when, Antoni, taking up a horn, blew it for some time.

The sound of the strong blast echoed through the dreary

caverns, and reverberated amidst these dark recesses of the rocks in lengthened peals: the sounds at length died away, in faint murmurs, and soon ceased to be heard.

De Clifford now heard the clanking of some massy chains, which appeared to be let down from above; and shortly the large gate began to creak on its strong hinges: as soon as it was sufficiently opened to permit the boat through, Antoni, when they had passed it, again blew the horn.—The chains now appeared to be drawn up, and De Clifford, looking back on the gate, beheld it slowly returning to its original position; and soon a dismal clank announced to him that it had again closed.

The cavern soon became gradually lighter, and the boat now emerged from those gloomy recesses, into an open place of some extent, but completely surrounded by immense and lofty rocks, amongst whose dark chasms grew many trees, which, bending over the sheet of water below, dipped their leafy branches in the smooth element.

CHAPTER VI.

> "Slaves, who ne'er knew mercy—
> Some unrelenting money-loving villains,
> Who laugh at human nature, and forgiveness,
> And are, like fiends, the factors for destruction."
>
> ROWE.

> "Thou hast a grim appearance,
> And thy face bespeaks command in it."
>
> SHAKESPEARE.

> "A deadly cold has froze the blood;
> The pliant limbs are stiff,
> And all the animating fire is quench'd."
>
> ROWE.

As the boat proceeded directly across the unruffled surface of the water, De Clifford surveyed the wonderful place he was in with great attention; he cast his eyes around the steep rocks which enclosed it, but could not discover any appearance of a castle, or outlet, by which they might leave it.

Sebastiano regarded De Clifford with an angry scowling look, and seemed to be contriving in his mind how he should revenge himself, for the wound he had received from him in his arm, which he was obliged to wear in a sling, and which gave him great pain.

The boat had now gained the opposite side of the rocks, when one of the men pushing aside the overhanging branches of a large tree, the boat glided on into a small cavern paved with large stones: on this the party stood, when they got out of the boat, and Antoni blew his horn.

The very singular sounds caused by it from above, made De Clifford look up, when, to his astonishment, he beheld a large circular tube, seemingly cut out of the solid rock: whilst he was gazing at this singular place, he beheld something moving, in the dusky recess, and at length discovered a large iron chair, which descended slowly down it, and at length rested on the pavement.

In this chair, which was large enough to hold three men, was De Clifford seated, with two of the banditti; and as soon as the horn gave the signal, it ascended through the tube, being drawn up by four large iron chains. For some time they were in complete darkness; at length a glimmering light was perceived from above; and, as the chair ascended, De Clifford saw some men with torches in their hands, looking down into the tube: the light glaring on their countenances, discovered a set of ferocious, blood-hardened features, as almost made him recoil with horror from the sight.

The chair, at length, came on a level with the stone floor of a large passage; and De Clifford beheld four men, two of whom held an iron handle, with which they turned round a beam, on which the chains that supported the chair were wound: the other two held the torches, to light their fellows to work.

De Clifford leaving the chair, with the two men, stood in the passage: the men welcomed their comrades on their return.

"Well, Pietro, what success have you had," said one of them, "and who is this stranger?" pointing to De Clifford.

"One that we must take care of," returned he:—"he has only wounded Sebastiano, and been the cause of the death of nine of our comrades."

"Has he, by saint Pedro?" said the other ruffian, "then I'll do his business."

The ruffian now rushed on De Clifford, and was drawing his dagger from his belt, when Pietro stept between them, and desired him, on pain of Sebastiano's displeasure, to desist.

The fellow, muttering a volley of curses, now drew back, and contented himself with reviling De Clifford in the bitterest terms.

De Clifford disdained to reply to the ruffian's abusive language, and with folded arms stood musing on his unhappy situation; and trusting in that guardian Providence, he had never intentionally offended, to protect him, he patiently, and with resignation, awaited the result.

The two men now unwinding the chains, the chair again descended; and when it returned, Sebastiano and Antoni appeared in it.

"Conduct the prisoner, Pietro and Gomelli," said the fierce Sebastiano, "to one of the lower dungeons, on the north side of the Castello, till we have time to punish him by the torturous rack, for the wound he gave me." He now passed on, and Pietro and Gomelli ordered De Clifford to follow them.

When he reached the end of the extensive passage, a folding portal appeared, which, being opened, De Clifford found himself in a large and lofty hall, in the shape of an octagon: on each side were doors, similar to the one through which he had passed: in the center of the hall stood a colossal statue of a man, in black marble, which was placed on a square pedestal, of the same materials.

In this hall the men stopped, and Pietro laying his torch on a

projecting corner of the pedestal, tied a bandage over De Clifford's eyes: one of them then taking him by the arm, led him
some paces forwards, and then turning round, directed him to
stoop his body, while he descended some steps—a door closed
on them; and when the men had arrived at the bottom of the
steps, they untied the bandage from De Clifford's eyes, who
found himself in a wide passage, which was lighted, at intervals,
with lamps.

This led into a lofty chamber, which was apparently below
the earth, as the light was admitted to it only by a sky-light in
the roof, from which descended a large iron lamp, which being
now lighted, throwing its rays around, discovered to De Clifford
a large table, by which sat more than forty desperate and ferocious ruffians; some of them were lying asleep, on the table, quite
inebriated; others were swearing and cursing each other, only
pausing while they were applying the flask to their mouths.

"Where's Bernardo?" roared out Pietro; "is he among you here?"

At the sound of his voice the whole gang started up, and
getting around, demanded all at once what success they had had
in their cruize, and where the rest of their comrades were?

"All that's left of them," said Pietro, "will soon be here, but we
threw nine overboard in an engagement."

Pietro having satisfied their enquiries about the names of
those who had been slain, and informed them that they had
taken a great deal of plunder, they returned again to the table,
seemingly so much contented with the spoils that had been
gained, that they did not seem in the least to lament the loss of
their comrades.

Bernardo, who had meanwhile been absent from the hall, now
appeared, and as he was approaching them, De Clifford could
not avoid taking notice of his gigantic figure, athletic make, and
savage countenance, which even surpassed, in ferocity, those of
the rest of the gang. In his belt, on one side, he wore two stillet-
toes, and a sword, and on the other side hung a bunch of large
keys.

"Well," said he, in a rough hollow voice, "what is to be done with this prisoner, for that's what you called me for, I suppose? has Sebastiano given any particular orders concerning him?" said he, looking significantly at Pietro and Gomelli.

"Not yet," returned Pietro, "but he said something about the torture to-morrow; however, I suppose you will get your orders respecting that; and for the present he is to be confined in one of the lower dungeons, under the north ramparts."

"Why, by San Marco, they are all full," said he.—"Stay—no, now I recollect, one of the fellows died this morning; but, as he has not been removed, you must come and help me."

Pietro and Gomelli both growled out an oath at this; however, it availed nothing, and they followed Bernardo and De Clifford, through many subterraneous passages; at length they descended some steps, at the bottom of which was a strong portal; this Bernardo unlocked, and they entered a passage, on both sides of which were several doors, strongly cased with iron.

Bernardo stopped at one of them, which he opened, and De Clifford entering the gloomy abode, started back with horror; for a pale, emaciated face, met his view; and the lifeless body of a man was laying stretched out on the ground.

"There," said Bernardo, "there he lays, dead enough; I almost fell over him this morning; however, I'm glad he's gone, for he was always sighing and groaning, and such like nonsense. I hope you," said he, turning to De Clifford, "won't be such a fool?"

De Clifford, wrapt up in horror, replied not, but continued gazing on the ghastly object before him.

"Come," said Bernardo, "do you two pull the body out, while I hold the torch."

"Ay, ay," said Gomelli, "let's have it done at once, for I want to get some wine; and indeed I think some of the others should have had this job, who have been stuffing here this last fortnight, while we have been hard at work."

"Cease your growling," roared Bernardo: "here, do you take up the legs, and Pietro take hold of the arms, and I'll light you."

Gomelli and Pietro reluctantly did as Bernardo ordered them; and when they had lifted up the body from the ground, asked him where it was to be carried to?

While in this attitude, the view that presented itself to De Clifford was more horrible than the weak pen can describe;—the savage countenance of the two ruffians, who were suspending the body from the ground; the wan ghastly face of the corpse hanging down, with the hair trailing on the earth; and the ferocious Bernardo, with his diabolical visage, giving them orders—formed a group, that no painter, however skilful, could give a just idea of.

Bernardo now told them to bear the body away, and he would shew them where to put it: they then retired, and closed the door on the unfortunate De Clifford, who was left in profound darkness.

CHAPTER VII.

"Virtue, when distress'd,
Can smile at death, and as a friend embrace it."

MARTYNS.

"But she, in mournful sounds, does still complain;
Sings all the night, tho' all her songs are vain!
And still renews the melancholy strain."

LEE.

"The ways of heaven, though
Dark, are just; and oft some guardian power
Attends unseen, to save the innocent."

DRYDEN.

DE CLIFFORD, wrapt up in melancholy ruminations, listened to the receding steps of the men, as they echoed along the vaulted passages.

Death was to him no object of horror, since he had lost his adored Matilda; but to lose his existence by the hands of a ferocious banditti, and by the torturous means of the rack, or other implements of cruelty, was more than he could look on, without shuddering with horror.

He prayed heaven to give him fortitude in these trying moments; and through the melancholy dreary night, he paced his dungeon, with a mind impressed with sad and painful emotions.

He was roused from the miserable reverie in which he was plunged, by the sound of a guitar, which appeared to be above him: he listened to some melancholy notes which were drawn from it, by a most exquisite performer; and the voice of a female who sung to it, now broke on the solemn silence that had reigned around.

The words were in Italian; and De Clifford, who perfectly understood that language, endeavoured to turn them into English, but which he found himself unable to do, without diminishing the native beauty of the author. They run thus—

> O Hope, seraphic maid, illume my soul;
> Peace to my woe-fraught mind restore:
> To me, in airy visions tell,
> If Rhinaldo I shall e'er see more.
>
> Guard him, ye Powers, from every ill,
> From dark despair, O keep his mind,
> And to his anxious bosom tell,
> His Laura ne'er will prove unkind.
>
> Faithful to him, I'll be till death
> Calls me to realms of bliss, on high;
> And with my latest quivering breath,
> Bless him until I speechless lie

This last line was concluded in such a plaintive, melancholy tone, that the big tears coursed each other down the pallid countenance of De Clifford; and doubly now did he regret his miserable situation, since it denied him the possibility of assisting the unfortunate Laura, who, like himself, was a wretched prisoner, in the power of the savage Sebastiano.

Again he desisted from pacing his dreary dungeon, and listened, in hopes the mournful musician would resume her dulcet harmony, but in vain—all was silent, the music had entirely ceased—and, disappointed, De Clifford leaned against the rough and craggy wall, absorbed in melancholy.

He was soon, however, disturbed, by hearing the horrid voice of Bernardo in the passage, saying, "here you, Breganto, hold the torch, whilst I unlock the door."

De Clifford now heard the key applied to the lock of his dungeon, which grated against the rusty wards, and the door creaking harshly on its hinges, the place was illumined by the light of the torch.

Bernardo now entered; "come Signor," said he, "you are wanted in the hall above."

De Clifford endeavoured to compose his internal agitations, and knowing resistance would be folly, quitted his cell, and entered the passage which was lighted by the torches; there he saw a party of the banditti, armed with long pikes, who awaited to conduct him to the place of torture.

Placing him in the midst of them, they traversed the long passages, and passed the large chambers, which the light of day, entering through the skylight, now illuminated with its bright beams.

Here the torch was extinguished, and when they had proceeded some time, through several passages, which, as on the preceding evening, were lighted by several lamps, De Clifford, again, had a bandage tied over his eyes; and, getting up the same narrow staircase he had descended the night before, he found himself, when the bandage was untied, again in the octagon hall, which was now full of the banditti, with Sebastiano and Antoni at their head.

De Clifford regarded the sanguinary and ferocious gang who were before him, without appearing moved or intimidated at their horrible appearance; while Sebastiano, with a look of malice and rage, commanded the tortures to be instantly prepared.

Antoni looked on, with manifest displeasure in his countenance, which De Clifford perceived, but well knowing that he could not kindle the feelings of pity or compassion in the obdurate breast of Sebastiano, without hesitation quietly submitted to his fate.

A rope was lowered from the roof of the hall, to which, at the end, two loops were fastened; into these loops were put the arms of De Clifford; a large weight was then tied to each of his legs; and in that condition he was drawn up into the air: the cords that were round his arm-pits, being drawn tight, caused the most acute sensations of agony to De Clifford, and an approving smile from the cruel and barbarous Sebastiano.

The sound of a distant horn now echoed through the passages of the Castello, at which Sebastiano, and the whole gang, rushed out of the hall. Antoni only remained behind, who instantly commanded the men who held the rope by which De Clifford was suspended, to let him gently down.

When this was done, he advanced to him, and with a countenance full of grief, said, "Signor, I wish it was in my power to serve you; believe me, I respect your bravery; and, should I have an opportunity, rely on my services."

He now left the hall, and De Clifford remained with the four men who had been ordered to torture him.

A profound silence now reigned in the hall for near an hour, when Antoni again entered; and, with pleasure in his countenance, informed De Clifford that Sebastiano had left the Castello, which was now under his command; and having ordered the cords to be taken off his arms, and the weights from his feet, ordered the four savage-looking wretches to quit the hall.

De Clifford now returned him his most grateful acknowledgements for his kind and generous conduct.

"Signor," said Antoni, "believe me, my heart has been afflicted at your suffering; but so revengeful is Sebastiano, he never forgives any one who opposes him, though even in a defence of their lives, liberty or property. The horn that you just now heard, proclaims some vessel in sight; and Sebastiano has taken the greatest part of the banditti with him—his return is uncertain: till he does revisit these walls, my power is absolute; nor shall you again return to your dungeon, until he arrives."

De Clifford pressed the hand of Antoni, for this great kindness; and, anxious to learn who the unfortunate female was, he demanded of him, if he knew any thing of her?

"No," replied Antoni, "I do not; that part of the Castello, which is under the charge of Bernardo, I never visit, by the particular orders of Sebastiano; his reason I am ignorant of, unless he thinks that I should upbraid him with his horrible acts of cruelty and oppression, towards his fellow-creatures. But, Signor," said he, "I forget that you very possibly are in need of refreshment; let me entreat you to accompany me to my apartments, where I shall be able to administer to your wants; and then I will, should you wish it, lead you round this impregnable fortress, which art and nature have contributed to render, perhaps, the strongest and most secure residence in the world."

De Clifford, who had not tasted any nourishment for many hours, accepted his kind invitation; and Antoni leading the way, he followed him through one of the portals, that opened from the hall into a large chamber, which, though in good preservation, was devoid of furniture.

Not seeing any other door or way of leaving this apartment, De Clifford looked round him with surprise.

Antoni remarked his wondering gaze, and said, "this Castle, Signor, was built by the father of the present owner of it; and is contrived so, that the communications from one part to another are entirely secret; and I believe there are few in the Castle, excepting Sebastiano and Bernardo, who are acquainted with the various passages which lead to the different parts.—It is now five years since I have unfortunately been here myself, and I know but few parts of it; however, Signor, I will now shew you one."

So saying, he advanced to a pillar, which was placed at one part of the chamber, apparently to support the roof; and touching a spring, a door flew open, and discovered a flight of steps. Antoni now bid De Clifford to descend them, who, having complied, soon arrived at the bottom, where he found himself in an apartment, furnished in the most sumptuous and elegant manner that the age afforded.

Unprepared for such a display of riches as appeared in this chamber, (by the desolate appearance of the room above), De Clifford expressed his admiration at it; but Antoni interrupted him, and with a sigh, said—

"Alas! Signor, what you see in this chamber has been got by force and rapine; and though you see me leagued with this ferocious banditti, yet, believe me, I am most averse to such a horrible way of passing my life—and would leave it this moment, if I could; but, to effect an escape from this place is impracticable, which you may well judge, from what you saw when you came to the Castello; for that is the only way there is to enter these walls; all other parts are inaccessible: no boats are ever allowed to be kept; and except when the brigantine is here, no one can go out—and then Sebastiano being in the Castello, renders it impossible; so that once within these walls, all hope of flight is denied. Here must I wear out my existence, unless, by some fortuitous circumstance, I may regain my liberty."

CHAPTER VIII.

"What is here?
Gold! yellow, glitt'ring, precious gold!
Thus much of this will make black white, foul fair,
Wrong right, base noble, old young, cowards valiant.
This yellow slave
Will knit and break religions, bless th'accurs'd,
Make the hoar leprosy ador'd, place thieves,
And give them title, knee, and approbation,
With senators on the bench."

SHAKESPEARE.

DE CLIFFORD now partook of some refreshment with the compassionate Antoni, who, when he had so done, invited him to walk round the Castle. "The fresh air," said he, "will revive you, after having been so long confined in the hold of the vessel."

De Clifford complied with Antoni's request; and, leaving the chamber they were in, by a sliding pannel, found himself in a passage, at the end of which was a door; this being opened, disclosed a large courtyard, surrounded with lofty walls.

Having crossed this, they wound up a long and tedious flight of stone steps; and at length arrived on an extensive terrace—here the uncommon lively view which presented itself to De Clifford, drew from him an exclamation of surprise.

On one side was seen the cerulean waves of the Mediterranean sea, and part of the Italian shores, which stretched out to the south; and on the east rose in majestic grandeur, the Alps, bounding the extensive prospect with their lofty summits, which were enveloped in the clouds; the Pyrenees also terminated the view, on the north and western side; and the intervening country appeared like a vast amphitheatre, surrounded by those lofty mountains, richly adorned with towns and villages, the spires of whose lofty churches and convents, piercing the umbrageous shades that surrounded them, caught the delighted eye, and by their pleasing variety, encreased the beauty of the scene.

De Clifford having contemplated this enchanting prospect for some time, with the greatest delight, Antoni led him to the south side of the Castello, and there pointed out to him the brigantine, which was getting under way.

A man now crossed them, who was habited in a short green jacket, and wore on his head a light helmet; in his hand he carried a pike, and by his side was slung a bugle-horn: when he passed Antoni, he lowered the end of his pike, in token of respect; and was continuing his walk, when Antoni demanded of him, where the vessel was that the brigantine was going in pursuit of?

The man pointed out a sail, which was apparently steering for the Gulph of Genoa, saying, "that is the vessel, Signor; but if our commander does not make haste, he will hardly overtake her. Have you any further commands, Signor?"

Antoni replying that he had none, the man then pursued his way—turning to De Clifford, "that man," said he, "was taken by Sebastiano, at the same time I was; and I believe, is as unwilling as myself to stay in this place: he is one of the light troops, whose business it is to procure provision from the country, when it is wanted; two of them are also continually stationed on these walls, to give notice of any vessel being in sight, and which happened so providentially to-day, in the moment when Sebastiano was putting in force his revengeful designs against you."

"I will now," continued he, "return to the Castle, and shew you the armoury belonging to it; and then, should you desire it, relate to you my history, which, though short, is pregnant with misfortunes!"—Here Antoni heaved a deep sigh; and De Clifford, whose own sad situation recurred to him, gave way to his grief.

Retracing now their way, they descended the long flight of steps, and again found themselves in the court-yard. Antoni opened the door that led to the passage; and from thence, touching a spring, the pannel drew back, and they were once more in Antoni's apartment: they now ascended the stairs, and opening the door in the column, they passed on into the octagon hall.

De Clifford now demanded of Antoni, who the black figure, that was placed in the center, was intended to represent?

"It is placed there," replied Antoni, "to perpetuate the memory of the founder of this Castello, and also serves another purpose, which you would little suspect."

Antoni now advanced to it, and touching a spring, a door flew open in the pedestal, and disclosed a flight of stairs—De Clifford immediately conceived that this was the place he descended, when he was blindfolded, and again, when he was brought up to receive the cruel punishment that was prepared: he however enquired of Antoni, if he was right in his conjectures?

"Yes," said Antoni, "this communicates with the residence of the banditti, and is the only mode they have of entering this part of the Castle, which is inhabited only by Sebastiano, Bernardo, and myself. In retired chambers, to which some of those doors lead, are the stores for the plunder and treasures, and also the armoury, which I am now going to shew you. You see, this Castle is so contrived, that should the banditti attempt to force this part, with any mutinous intent, they could only do it singly; and they have no arms below, so that a few would easily withstand them; and this passage is always secured at night."

So saying, he passed on, and opening one of the folding doors, De Clifford beheld an immense hall, which was converted into an armoury, completely stored with all kinds of weapons, offensive and defensive; the walls were hung round with coats of armour, spears, helmets, battle-axes, shields, swords, darts, stilettos, and bows and arrows—in short, every weapon which was in use in those days. De Clifford could not help admiring the very excellent order in which every thing was disposed.

Antoni, after he had shewn every part of this place to De Clifford, said, "I will now, Signor, shew you where a part of the treasures are deposited; I say part, for Sebastiano has many other stores, of which I am ignorant; they are only known to himself and Bernardo, who is his confidant; but by what I shall let you see, you will be able to form an idea, how successful he has been in his hardy enterprises."

They now left the armoury, and Antoni opened another of the doors, before which appeared a flight of steps; ascending this, they entered a small room, which had a door on one side; this Antoni opened, and bid De Clifford stand close by his side: he then pulled a rope, and the part of the floor they stood on slowly descended, till it touched the marble pavement of a hall, equal in size to the armoury, in which were bales of merchandize, filled up on all sides; they passed through this, and entered into the apartment, which was full of large chests, which were completely filled with gold and silver coin, and bars of those precious metals.

The sight of so much treasure surprised De Clifford, for in these two halls were contained what would purchase whole provinces.

"These stores," said Antoni, "which you now behold, as I before informed you, constitute a part only of what the Castello contains, as I have heard Sebastiano declare; of what use they can be to him, I will leave you, Signor, to judge—for them, has he bartered his peace of mind and repose, and lives in these gloomy walls, amid a crew of the most ferocious and sanguinary wretches, that perhaps the world contains; and though secure in this impenetrable fortress, yet he is a stranger to the blessings of an undisturbed slumber: indeed, were the holy brotherhood even to enter the place, and were they to penetrate as far as the octagon hall, they would never be able to discover the secret recesses, into which, in such a time of danger, the banditti would conceal themselves, and would so bewilder themselves, in the intricate turnings and windings, that they would become an easy prey to the banditti."

"In what manner," said De Clifford, "was the large iron grate opened, that defends the passage of the caverns from the further progress of any boats, and where you first blew the horn?"

"As the day is not much spent," said Antoni, "I will shew you how that is effected. That barrier is, indeed, of itself, a sufficient defence against an approach; but united with that afforded by the iron chair, which will not allow more than three to ascend, completes the security."

They now approached the platform, on which they descended into these magazines of the plunder of the banditti; and when they stood on it, Antoni pulled a rope, and it ascended to its original station; and they once more arrived in the octagon hall.

Antoni crossed to the opposite side, and opened another door, which led into a long passage, lighted at the top of the sides of the walls by loop-holes; through this they proceeded a long way, over uneven ground, and at length emerged from those damp places, into the open air; and climbing over some of the rough and craggy rocks, at last entered a stone building.

In this sat six of the savage banditti, round a misshapen table, on which was placed several flasks of wine. They all arose when Antoni entered, who desired them to re-seat themselves, as he only wanted to see the state of the works which moved the iron grating below.

So saying, he passed on, and entered an opposite chamber, where De Clifford saw a large iron wheel, round which was an immense chain, of the same metal; the wheel was fixed on an axle, which was supported on the two sides by blocks of wood, and to both ends of which was a large handle.

"The way it is managed," said Antoni, "is simply this—by a particular wind of the horn, the men know whether the gate is to be opened or shut, and which is done by turning the wheel either backwards or forwards, as you perceived when you passed through it."

De Clifford expressed his thanks to Antoni, for the great attention and kindness he had shewn him: and they now pursued their way back, through the long passage, and at length arrived in Antoni's apartment, by means of the hollow column.

When they were seated there, De Clifford pressed Antoni

to relate to him the manner in which he became an inmate of the dreary Castello De Strombolo, and had attained the present rank he held in it.

Antoni, who seemed to be suddenly affected by some remembrances, was, for a short period, silent; but at length he appeared to collect his spirits, and thus commenced the promised recital of the events of his life.

CHAPTER IX.

The Narrative of Antoni.

"Love, the most gen'rous passion of the mind—
The softest refuge innocence can find;
The safe director of unguided youth,
Fraught with kind wishes, and secur'd by truth;
The cordial drop heaven in our cup has thrown,
To make the nauseous draught of life go down."

ROCHESTER.

THE adventures of my life, Signor, are scarcely worthy your attention; but, as I feel myself in some measure called on to state to you by what means I became an inmate of Strombolo, I shall briefly relate the singular circumstances which produced that event.

I shall pass over the first eighteen years of my life, and commence at a circumstance which was the origin of them. My name is Antoni Rhinaldo; my father is a Venetian senator, and possessed of considerable property. I resided principally in Venice, and used to amuse myself in the evening, by attending the casinos, or in water-parties.

One night as I was returning home, after an excursion on the water, I saw two men concealing themselves, behind some large columns which supported a portico: my attention was engaged by this circumstance; and I took a position, where I could not be easily perceived, to watch their motions.

After I had waited about a quarter of an hour, a carriage

passed along, and I beheld the two men rush out; one of them wounded the driver, and the other, opening the door of the carriage, dragged out a lady, who appeared to have fainted with excess of terror; and bearing her in his arms, carried her off—I instantly followed him at a short distance, and saw him place the lady in a gondola, and rowed off with his prize. I immediately jumped into one, which I fortunately found, and followed him as near as I could, without hazarding observation.

After rowing some time, he passed into a canal, which led to an unfrequented part of the suburbs, and stopping at a mean-looking house, gave a shrill whistle.

The door soon opened, and an old woman appeared, who, descending the steps that led to the water, assisted the man to force the lady up them. I thought I heard her attempt to scream several times, and so concluded that they had gagged her. The door of the house now closed, and in a short time the man came out, and stepping into the gondola, returned the same way he came.

I now lay down in my boat, until he had passed me, and then I rowed to the house, determined, if possible, to rescue the lady from the dangers with which she was surrounded. I placed the gondola close under the windows of the house, and could plainly hear the lady moaning in a most lamentable manner, and the old woman talking to her.

I now muffled my face up in my cloak, and ascending the steps, knocked softly at the door—presently the old woman opened it.—"Is she arrived?" said I, in a low voice.

"Yes, Signor," said the old hag, "Gonrez brought her here about a quarter of an hour ago."

"I wonder how I missed him," said I, in the same whisper: "do you go down and secure the gondola, while I visit her."

I now hastily passed her, and opened the door of the room I had reason to believe she was in.

As soon as she saw me enter, she hid her face in her garments, and screamed out with affright.

"Detested barbarian!" said she, "do not think to gain your vile ends, which I will sooner die than submit to."

"Signora," said I, uncovering my face, "look at me; behold in me your deliverer: I saw you seized and dragged from your carriage, and have followed you to this place, where I have been so fortunate as to gain admittance. Do not, I beseech you, doubt either my word or my honour, which I pledge to you, that I will restore you safe to your home and friends, if fortune will so far favour me."

Surprised at my discourse, the lady uncovered her face, and looked on me while I was addressing her.

If before I had seen her face I felt interested, and determined to risk my life for her safety, how much more did I feel inclined so to do, when I beheld one of the most lovely, most beautiful women that my eyes ever gazed on!—She was apparently about eighteen; her lovely dark eyes, that were raised up to me with gratitude, for my intentions, stole my heart. The veil that she had wore, had been torn off, in her efforts to resist the fell designs of the wretches in whose power she had fallen, and shewed her dark ringlets, which were confined on the back of her head by strings of pearls, except some few locks which had escaped, and which wantoned on her snowy neck and bosom. She now, with evident emotion, addressed me, and while she was so doing, displayed the most lovely teeth I had ever beheld. She was indeed made for a Venus.

"Signor," said she, "I cannot be too grateful to you for your goodness. I am indeed now threatened with the most horrible dangers: trusting to your honour, I will commit myself to your protection; but alas! I fear it is too late, as the base contriver of this cruel plot is expected here every moment."

I said no more, but immediately assisted her to rise from her seat; and having requested she would shew a reluctance to follow me, we went out of the room.

The old woman, who had, in the mean time, been busied in securing the gondola, was now returning; she seemed extremely surprised to see me leave the house.

"How, Signor," said she; "I thought you intended to—"

"No, no," said I, hastily interrupting her, "I have changed my mind. Come, Signora," said I, addressing myself to the lady, whilst we descended the steps, "if you will not come quietly, I shall be necessitated to use force."—However, to be brief, we got into the gondola, which I instantly unloosed, and, with a palpitating heart, pushed off from the house.

As there was every reason to suppose that we should meet the author of this dark act, I immediately crossed to the opposite side of the canal, and rowed off, as fast as my strength would permit.

Soon, however, the silence of the night was interrupted, by the dashing of oars in the water; and I perceived a gondola, with some men in it, swiftly advancing.

I immediately desired the lady to lay down in the bottom of the boat, whilst I began, with seeming unconcern, to sing a popular song, and apparently rowed at leisure.

My plan succeeded admirably—the men conceiving that I was one of the gondoliers, hailed me as they passed, and wished me a good-night; I returned the same to them, and then continued my song, rowing now as fast as I could, for the moments were indeed precious.

I now demanded of the lady, who had almost fainted, with the great agitation she suffered, in what part of the city she resided? she replied, in a faint and trembling voice—"Near the church of San Marco."

"Then," said I, "Signora, it will be the safest for us to pursue an opposite direction; for, doubtless, when they miss you, they will instantly steer towards that part, in the hopes of overtaking you, and by that means I may be disappointed in the happiness of being the preserver of your honour."

"Use your own judgment," replied the lady, "only preserve me from falling into the power of Rugantino."

"Sooner than that should happen, Signora," said I, "I would willingly sacrifice my life: be not alarmed; the saints, I trust, will protect you from him."

We now turned out of the canal, and, as I had determined, proceeded far from the direction of the colonnades of Saint Mark.

I directed my course towards the Adriatic, conceiving that it would be least imagined that we could have taken that route.

The beams of the morning now began to appear in the east, and soon the curling surface of the sea reflected the radiance of the rising sun. With pleasure I perceived the market boats at a distance; and now, weary with the great fatigue I had undergone, for the first time lay on my oars.

The roses in the downy cheeks of the beautiful Signora now began to return, and pleasure at being so wonderfully preserved, beamed in her lovely eyes.

It was with the utmost difficulty that I could refrain from falling at her feet, and confessing the ardent passion I felt; but, however, the delicacy of her situation prevented me; and when unperceived, I gazed on those charms that captivated my soul, I drank deep draughts of love.

As I had great hopes that now all danger was over, as the boats began to glide along the smooth surface of the canals, I now turned my gondola and directed my course for San Marco—and seeing that the lady had greatly recovered her spirits, I requested that she would inform me of the circumstances which occasioned the violent plans that had been employed to secure her person.

"I should be most ungrateful, Signor," returned the lady, "if, after the signal services you have rendered me, and which can never be obliterated from my breast, I could refuse to satisfy your curiosity in that respect; and shall, with pleasure, relate to you the cause of my being carried off to that place, from whence you so generously rescued me."

———

A heavy foot was now heard pacing the chamber above, and Antoni starting up, said to De Clifford, "I must leave you, Signor, for a short time, as Bernardo is come to place the centinels for the night, and to secure the different passages of the Castello."

So saying, he departed up the spiral staircase, which led through the column, to the apartment above; and De Clifford soon after heard them quit the place.

CHAPTER X.

"The saffron morn, with early blushes spread,
Now rose refulgent, from Tithonus' bed,
With new-born day, to gladden mortal sight,
And gild the courts of heaven with sacred light."

POPE.

"So dear to heaven is sainted Charity,
That when a soul is found sincerely so,
A thousand livery'd angels lacquey her,
Driving far off each thing of sin and guilt."

MILTON.

WHEN Antoni returned, he made an apology to De Clifford for leaving him, and observing that it was time to refresh themselves, placed on the table some provisions.

When the wants of nature had been supplied, Antoni thus addressed De Clifford:—

"Signor," said he, "from the miserable abodes you have had lately, you must stand in need of repose: it now grows late— to-morrow I will resume my narrative."

De Clifford, who, in listening to the adventures of Antoni, for a while forgot the poignancy of his grief, and the horror of his situation, thankfully acquiesced in his wishes; and being weary, from the miserable night he had lately passed, threw himself on a couch in the room, when sleep soon lulled him to a short forgetfulness of woe.

When he awoke in the morning, the beams of the sun illumined the chamber—Antoni was not in the room, but he saw him soon after enter it, through the sliding pannel.

De Clifford, refreshed with the repose he enjoyed, partook of the morning's repast with appetite.

"As the morning is so fine and serene," said Antoni, "would you, Signor, like to ascend to the terrace, where I will continue the relation I began last night?"

De Clifford consented with pleasure, and leaving the apartment with Antoni, ascended the numerous steps which led to the terrace, where, seated on the projecting rocks, Antoni thus continued:—

———————

I believe I left off, Signor, where the beautiful Signora was going to relate to me how she came in the situation I found her.

"My parents," said she, "are the Marchese and Marchesa De Palmyra, whose pallazio is near the church of San Marco."

"I know them well," I replied, "but, till this period, was ignorant of the inestimable jewel which they possessed in you, Signora."

She blushed at these words, and then continued.—"It is now hardly three weeks, Signor, since I left the Convent where I was educated, which perhaps is the reason. About six months ago, on the eve of the Annunciation, when we were performing the religious service in the chapel, I observed a man, who had taken his station near the grate, remain with his eyes fixed on me, during the whole of the time.

"He was a tall figure, well dressed, of a commanding and ferocious aspect. I felt uncommonly distressed at the circumstance, and was glad when the ceremony was ended. I observed that the cavalier was the last to depart the chapel, and even while he was so doing, still kept his eyes on me.

"The next morning, the first who came into the chapel was this person—he again took his station in the same place, where he remained until he was obliged to depart, the service being concluded.

"The Convent had a most delightful garden, and in it I used generally to walk every evening, to enjoy the cool reviving air.

"According to custom, I was straying through the beautiful mazes which adorned it, on the evening of that day, when suddenly I heard some voices in an arbour behind me.—Conceiving it was some of the boarders who were there, I turned round, and soon found myself in the arms of the cavalier whom I had observed so intently noticing me in the church.

"You may easily, Signor, (said she,) imagine my agitation—I screamed most violently with affright—but all was in vain: the cavalier bore me away to a distant part of the garden, where two other men joined him: they quickly raised a ladder against the wall of the garden, when I beheld lights approaching us in various directions, from the Convent: rejoiced at this circumstance, I again exerted my voice—and the men, now seeing it was impossible to carry me off unperceived, quitted me and fled.

"The servants belonging to the Convent now assisted me to return to it; for my affright had been so great, that I was unable to walk without aid, and for a few days was confined to my room, through illness. Who it was that had made the daring attempt, I knew not, nor did I recollect ever having seen the cavalier, before the eve of the Annunciation. Some time passed, and, by degrees, I began to forget the circumstance—but I was fearful again to renew my evening walks in the Convent gardens, lest I might again be exposed to the danger I had so happily escaped.

"Very early one morning, the portress came to my apartment, and informed me that the Marchese, my father, was arrived. As I did expect to see him that day, I instantly followed her; but instead of going to the parlour, I remarked that she took a contrary direction, and demanded the reason?

'The Marchese, your father, Signora,' replied the portress, 'was fearful of disturbing the Lady Abbess, so instead of entering into the Convent, he is now awaiting in his carriage, at the north postern, as he has not time to get out, being obliged to return directly.'

"Unsuspectingly I followed the portress, who led me through a long passage, and opening a door, I saw what I conceived to be my father's carriage, and a domestic opening the door, I sprung into it to embrace him.

"Imagine my horror, when I again found myself strongly held by the same cavalier; who had before attempted to carry me off: the door of the carriage was instantly closed, and the horses were driven with the greatest velocity. I screamed, I raged, I tore my hair, and with tears beseeched him to release me, but in vain.

'Forgive,' said he, 'Signora, the successful plan of a man who loves you to distraction, and who finds it impossible to exist without you. Calm,' said he, 'beautiful Signora, the emotions of your grief—whatever wealth can purchase, or invention form to please, shall be yours; look only on Rugantino with affection.'

'Forbear,' said I, 'to insult my ears with your infamous addresses, calculated only to encrease the horror and detestation I feel at the sight of you.'

"I had now been near an hour in the carriage, which had pro-ceeded with the greatest velocity, when at a distance I perceived the retinue of my father approaching. As soon as he came near me, I started up in the carriage suddenly, and said, 'Oh my father, protect, preserve your daughter, from the base designs of a vil-lain.'

"Rugantino instantly stopped my mouth, and dragged me back in the carriage, which was soon, almost immediately, stopped. He instantly jumped out, and shortly after the door on the opposite side was opened, and I found myself in my dear father's arms: he carried me to his own carriage, and we set off directly.

'Heaven be praised,' said he, 'that you are safe—I trust my people will not let the villain escape; but so anxious was I to get you from that scene of blood and horror, that I would not wait the issue, but seizing the first opportunity that presented itself, departed with you—but,' said he, 'relate to me how it was that you came to be in the situation I found you.'

"I related to him every circumstance, and when I had done

so, we arrived at the Convent. My father immediately related to the Abbess the circumstance; and desired that the portress, who, it evidently appeared, had been bribed to betray me, should be immediately brought to justice: it was, however, too late, for she had fled, and could no where be found.

"The domestics of my father now arrived, and stated to him that they had slain two of the ruffians, but that the principal had escaped.

"The Marchese instantly dispatched a messenger, to acquaint the officers of justice with the circumstance, in hopes that they would be able to apprehend him; but unfortunately he eluded their search.

"He now acquainted the Abbess with his determination to withdraw me instantly from the Convent—fearful lest another attempt should be made to carry me off, and which might meet with the desired success.

"I accordingly returned back to the Pallazio De Palmyra, with the Marchese. On the road was still standing the carriage in which Rugantino had attempted to carry me away; it was exactly painted to resemble the one my father usually travelled in, and which had so entirely deceived me, that I entered it without the smallest suspicion or idea of the cruel design that was formed against my honour; and had it not so happened that my father had seen me on the road, a circumstance that, with all his cunning, Rugantino had not foreseen, or perhaps was ignorant of the road he travelled, he would certainly have succeeded in his daring attempts.

"But, however, as you know, Signor, (continued the lady) he did not stop there. I had been near three weeks at my father's Pallazio, to which I was returning from a party, where I had passed the evening, when you so providentially witnessed his further plans to get me in his power, and saved me in a manner so wonderful, that I can scarcely yet believe it real. My parents, Signor, and myself, will endeavour to repay your kindness with unceasing gratitude."

So saying, the lovely female concluded her relation, and soon after we saw the lofty colonnades of San Marco, and I had the happiness of delivering her safe into the hands of her delighted parents.

Nothing could exceed their joy, or the thanks with which they loaded me, for the part I had taken for the preservation of their daughter, and entreated me to become a constant visitor at their Pallazio.

When I left them, I went to the house where the Signora Palmyra had been taken, but it was totally deserted; nor could I learn any intelligence of the old woman, who, had I found, would probably have discovered the residence of Rugantino, whom I most anxiously longed to bring to justice, for his atrocious acts; but notwithstanding all my endeavours to trace him, they proved ineffectual.

CHAPTER XI.

"Time gives encrease to my afflictions:
The circling hours, that gather all the woes
Which are diffus'd through the revolving year,
Come heavy laden, with the oppressing weight,
To me! with me successively they leave
The sighs, the tears, the groans, the restless cares,
And all the damps of grief that did retard their flight."

CONGREVE.

It was impossible to see the beautiful Signora Palmyra without loving her—and I soon found my heart irrevocably possessed by the tender passion: to be brief, Signor, in a short time I made a declaration of my sentiments to the idol of my affections—and had the happiness to perceive that they were favourably received by her.

My father, to whom I imparted the situation of my heart, undertook to solicit an alliance with his old friend the Marchese, and at length succeeded.

Nothing could exceed my joy and delight, at receiving the hand of my adored Laura—the days flew away on the wings of unutterable bliss, but, alas! brought on too soon the weary moments of despair and misery I am now condemned to suffer.—

Here Antoni stopped, overwhelmed with grief: De Clifford, who reverenced his sorrow, forbore to disturb him, and, catching the infection, was alike wrapt up in melancholy ruminations, on the loss of his adored Matilda.

At length Antoni recovered himself, and continued his recital.—After I had been married near a year, a distant relation died, and bequeathed to me his property which he possessed in Spain. It became necessary for me to go and take possession of the estates; and leaving my adored Laura with many tears, and a fatal foreboding of some calamity, I embarked for the Spanish coast.

We had not been long at sea, when, to our agonized sight, appeared a Barbary corsair, who immediately chased us: we prepared to defend ourselves, well knowing that death was preferable to slavery.

The vessel now fast approached us, when, to our unspeakable joy, we beheld a brigantine bearing down on the corsair, and instantly attack her: we were at a very small distance, and soon saw, to our sorrow, that the brigantine was in the greatest danger of being taken: I therefore exhorted the men to assist her, which they were the more ready to do, knowing that they would be taken themselves immediately, should the brigantine be defeated.

They therefore laid the vessel alongside the brigantine, and we entered it at the moment that the Moors had also boarded it. The first thing I beheld was the commander of the brigantine wounded, and on the point of becoming a victim to the furious Moors—I rushed on the savage, and instantly killed him.

It so happened that this man was the commander of the corsair; and the rest, seeing his fate, drew back, and soon delivered themselves up to our mercy.

Sebastiano, for he it was whose life I had saved, when he

returned to his senses, surveyed me for some time with attention; I was surprised at this circumstance, for of him I had no recollection, nor did I know that I had ever seen him before.

When he awoke from the depth of thought into which the sight of me seemed to have plunged him, he expressed his thanks to me, for having preserved his life, and entreated that I would not, for that evening, quit his vessel; this I complied with; and after the Moors had been confined, and order again restored in the vessels, I retired with him to his cabin, where we refreshed ourselves after the toils of the day.

Sebastiano pressed me so earnestly not to leave the vessel till the next morning, that I could not refuse his solicitations, and laying down on a couch in the cabin, passed the night on it.

The next morning when I arose, I went on deck; but what was my astonishment to find that my vessel had sailed off during the night, and now was nearly out of sight!

I instantly rushed down into the cabin, and, full of horror, related the circumstance to Sebastiano, who heard me calmly, and then, with a savage smile, said, "Signor, I owe you so much gratitude for past favours, that I cannot think of losing your society; we are now steering for my residence, where I shall be able to entertain you more agreeably than in this vessel." It was to no purpose for me to remonstrate—my vessel was gone, and I was forced to comply.

Sebastiano now informed me that he was the leader of a set of brave fellows, who, with himself, had admired my courage, and had come to him to propose that I should succeed the second in command, who had been slain in the engagement.

I saw I had no other resource at the present moment, and in hopes that I should soon be able to make my escape, accepted the situation.

We now arrived before the rocks, in whose dark recesses this Castle is built, in which, when I arrived, I was received by the rest of the banditti, as successor to the man who had been killed.

The horrid scenes I have witnessed since that period, are

more dreadful than the tongue can relate. I soon found out, that to escape was impossible, and for many months resigned myself to the most intense grief; at last I thought, that if I accompanied Sebastiano in his predatory excursions, that I should have more chance of effecting my designs, than if I immured myself in these horrid walls; but have found it as yet totally impracticable.

Thus, Signor, have I related to you the manner in which I have become an inhabitant of this detested place, where I fear I am destined to pine away my miserable existence, far from my friends, and from my wife, my adored Laura!—Oh wretched Rhinaldo, when will thy sorrows cease!

———————

De Clifford having expressed his thanks to Antoni, for the relation of his adventures, said, "It is strange, Signor, that when I was confined in the dungeon, on the first night of my arrival here, by order of Sebastiano, that the female voice which I heard, pronounced the name of Rhinaldo, as well as that of Laura; but you say you do not know any prisoners who are confined there."

"No," replied Antoni, "Sebastiano drew from me a promise that I would not visit that part of the Castello. I am ignorant of his reason, unless it proceeded from the little comforts I used to provide for the wretched inhabitants of those dreary dungeons, contrary to his will.

"That part of the Castle is kept by Bernardo, who is his firm friend; and as I could not have visited the prisoners without his knowledge, as he keeps the keys, I forbore to do it, rather than create any quarrel, which would only serve to render my situation more wretched: however, what you have informed me has roused my curiosity—and I am determined to find out, if possible, who the female is whom you heard sing. At present, Signor, we will return to my apartment, when, if it should so please you to recount your adventures to me, you will confer an obligation on the unfortunate Antoni."

When they were seated in the chamber, De Clifford complied with his wish, and related his melancholy tale.

The two friends mutually condoled each other; and thus the time past, till Antoni was warned to depart, by the approach of Bernardo.

"I have been thinking, Signor," said he, to De Clifford, when he returned, "that we will delay our intended visit to the dungeons, till the dawn of the approaching morning; for, as the unhappy object of our researches will perhaps be asleep, we shall not be able to learn who she is, till such time as she breaks on the sullen silence around, with her sad dulcet strains."

De Clifford acquiesced in this arrangement, and they passed the intervening hours in projecting schemes for their escape from Strombolo, all of which appeared alike impossible to carry into effect, since the only way they could ever pass the grate was by water, and there was no boat to enable them to do it.

At the first dawn of the morning they left the chamber, and ascending the terrace, proceeded round the Castle, till they came opposite to the north side of the building.

Here it was that the dungeons were: that in which De Clifford had been confined was under ground; the other rose over it. Between the terrace and the castle wall was a deep chasm in the rock, so that they could not approach to that part; they therefore were necessitated to watch the several gratings of the prison windows, to try if they could see the unhappy inmates; but the walls were of such a thickness, as to render it impossible to discover any thing in those gloomy abodes.

As it was yet very early, they continued their walk, and ascending a high rock, by some rough steps that were cut on its rugged side, they had an unconfined view of the blue waves of the Mediterranean.

No vessel met their enquiring eyes, a circumstance which gave great comfort both to Antoni and De Clifford, who indeed awaited the return of Sebastiano with agonizing sensations, as he would then be fated to endure the tortures his savage and malicious disposition would prepare for him.

When they had, for some time, viewed the vast expanse, and beheld the sun rising in majestic splendour, out of the bosom of the restless ocean, they retraced their steps down the side of the lofty rock, and took their station on that part of the terrace which faced the north side of the gloomy walls of Strombolo, anxious to hear if the melancholy songstress, who beguiled the dull and monotonous hours of her captivity with her plaintive laments, would at this early hour resume her harmonious occupation.

With their eyes fixed on the dark frowning walls, the two friends, seated on a projecting stone, in melancholy converse, beguiled the tedious hours.

CHAPTER XII.

"Think you behold him, like a raging lion,
Pacing the earth, and tearing up his steps;
Fate in his eyes, and roaring with the pain
Of burning fury."

OTWAY.

"His breast with fury burn'd, his eyes with fire,
Mad with despair."

DRYDEN.

THEY had been thus seated for some time, when their attention was suddenly attracted, by the notes of a guitar, and soon after De Clifford heard the same sweet voice sing the following song, in the Italian language:—

How tedious pass the lengthen'd hours,
    Bereft of liberty!
O give to me, ye heavenly powers!
    My own fond love to see.

On fierce Sebastiano's head,
    Let Laura's wrongs descend;
Let soft repose desert his bed,
    Who thus my heart does rend.

O where, Rhinaldo, dost thou stay?
    Ah! whither art thou gone?
O why to rescue me delay,
    A prisoner forlorn?

"Merciful powers!" exclaimed Antoni, starting up, "it is my wife—my Laura—it is her sweet voice—a prisoner too—and in Sebastiano's power—Oh God! 'tis too much!"—Here, with a lengthened groan, he fell on the terrace.

De Clifford raised him up, and with great difficulty recalled his fleeting senses. "Am I awake," said he, "or is what I have now heard but a dream?—tell me, my friend, while I have power to hear you."

De Clifford comforted the distracted Antoni, as much as was in his power—"We will escape," said he, "from this horrible Castle—we will free your Laura from her confinement, and you will yet be happy. Would to God," said he, "that I had the same bright prospect you have; but my adored Matilda is gone for ever, and beyond the power of man to recall."

Antoni at length began to be more composed, and again listened to hear the voice, but all was silent; nor could they conceive from which of the chambers the sounds came. With the utmost scrutiny they surveyed the dark walls, when the tones of the guitar again caught the ear, and directed them to a casement that was larger than the rest, and which was open; they listened for a while, and became convinced that the sounds proceeded from thence. De Clifford, fearful they might be observed, now intreated Antoni to leave the place, and to consult on the means to liberate his Laura, ere Sebastiano arrived.

At that name Antoni's eyes gleamed with fury, and lifting up his hands to heaven, he swore to be revenged on him for his cruel wrongs.

As they were retracing their way back to Antoni's apartment, they beheld the same man on the walls they had met two days before. "That man," said Antoni, "I am certain, would assist us in our schemes: I know his stay here is as unpleasant to him as mine is to myself, and I am determined that he shall be acquainted with our intentions;"—so saying, as he was passing them, Antoni beckoned to him to follow them.

The man instantly obeyed, and when they had arrived at his apartment, Antoni said, "Have you a wife, or a family, which you would wish to see?"

"Yes, Signor," the man sorrowfully replied, "I have a wife, and two children; it is now five years since I saw them; heaven knows what is become of them, or how my Annetta has borne the loss of her poor Carlo."

"Doubtless," said Antoni, "if you love her, you would undertake the most difficult enterprize to see her, and to leave this Castello."

"Oh Signor," said Carlo, "what is it you allude to? alas, you know it is impossible for any one to escape these walls; nor do I know what to think of your conversation."

"I mean," said Antoni, "if you are willing, to assist you in making your escape."

"To make my escape!" said Carlo, and fell on his knees. "O Signor, do that, and Carlo is your slave for ever."

"Rise," said Antoni; "what you have to perform is difficult indeed—but before I say more to you, swear by the blessed saints, that you will, as far as you are able, perform whatever it is found necessary that you should do."

Carlo joyfully took the oath required, and then was admitted into the consultation with De Clifford and Antoni; the result of which was, that Carlo should be let down in the iron chair, by De Clifford and Antoni, having with him a plank to assist to float him over the water; that, at a certain time, Antoni would, on some pretence, have the grate opened, which, when Carlo had passed, he would have no great difficulty to encounter; for, as soon as he should immerge from the caverns, he might effect a landing on the rocks, from whence he was to proceed to Venice, and there to request the assistance of the holy brotherhood; that when they had arrived near the Castello, he should make a signal, at a place pointed out; and that at the middle of the next night, they should proceed in their boats, under the rocks, and wait at the grate, which they would contrive to open for them; and that they would let down the chair, by which three of the party would be able to ascend, who could then assist their comrades to enter the Castle; and then Antoni and De Clifford would instruct them in what further they were to do to get possession of it.

Carlo listened attentively to his instructions, and then

professed his willingness to undergo any hardships and difficulties to effect the plan in view.

When the evening approached, and a dusky gloom began to pervade the face of nature, Carlo appeared prepared for his desperate undertaking, and with De Clifford and Antoni, silently paced the passage that led to the tube; he had provided a plank to bear himself up in the water, and accompanied by the prayers of De Clifford and Antoni, was lowered down by them in the iron chair.

Antoni and De Clifford then returned to their apartment, and beguiled the time in conversation, till the heavy steps of Bernardo were heard above: Antoni started up, and immediately went with him round the Castle, to see that all was secure for the night; and then expressed a wish to see if the men at the wheel were attentive to their duty, as he affected to think it likely that Sebastiano might arrive during the night; and then proceeded there with Bernardo.

When they had got to the place, Antoni appeared to examine the iron-work attentively; and, on pretence of seeing if all was in good order, made the men move it backwards and forwards several times: he knew that by this time Carlo would have arrived at it—and on this depended all his hopes.

When at length he had seen that every thing was in good order, he left the place, and rejoined De Clifford, who was anxiously awaiting him, and there related what he had done.

Should it so have happened that Carlo had not reached the grate, at the time it was opened, the poor fellow must inevitably perish, as it was impossible for him to return; and this idea contributed greatly to add to their anxiety, as on him all their hopes depended.

After a night passed in sleepless agitation, Antoni determined again to go to the wheel, and have it turned round, that should Carlo not have passed the grate, he would now have an opportunity.

Full of the idea, he the next morning, ere De Clifford had

risen, went to that post, and again had the grate opened.

Four days had now elapsed since Sebastiano had left the Castello De Strombolo: his return, when he went out on a cruise, was always uncertain; but was seldom longer than a fortnight, unless detained by unforeseen events.

Should Carlo succeed in his undertaking, they might expect him back in a week, when Sebastiano might still be absent; and having a large part of the banditti with him, would render their designs more easy to be accomplished.

The absence of Carlo was noticed the next day, and information of it given to Antoni, who immediately ordered every part of the Castle to be searched; and when the men could discover no traces of him, it was concluded that he had fallen down some of the precipices, and thus had perished; no one entertaining the least idea of his escape, as it was supposed a thing impracticable.

Antoni now, with De Clifford, would pass most of their time on the terrace, which fronted the north side of the Castello, in which was the dungeon of the unfortunate Laura.

From the thickness of the wall of her prison, it was impossible for her to see the top of the terrace, on which Antoni used to pace throughout the day; and on which he would stop to listen to the dulcet notes which she drew from her guitar, with which she used to beguile her melancholy hours.

Not knowing who might inhabit the other chambers, he was fearful of taking any steps by which he might make himself known to his adored Laura, lest it should come to the knowledge of Bernardo; who, if Sebastiano arrived before Carlo returned, would doubtless inform him of that circumstance: and Antoni now too plainly perceived the reason that made Sebastiano extort a promise from him, never to visit that part of the Castello; as, had he done so, he would probably have discovered the situation of his wife.

Frequently would he direct his eyes to the point on which Carlo was to make the signal when he returned; and frequently would he ascend the steep steps in the rock, to look whether there was any appearance of Sebastiano's brigantine. Six days had now elapsed since Carlo had been absent, and which his anxiety made appear to him as an age of weary expectancy.

CHAPTER XIII.

"If it were now to die,
'Twere now to be most happy:
My soul hath her content so absolute,
That not another comfort, like to this,
Succeeds in unknown fate."

SHAKESPEARE.

"My plenteous joys,
Wanton in fullness, seek to hide themselves
In drops of sorrow."

SHAKESPEARE.

THE seventh day approached; and De Clifford, with Antoni, were anxiously looking out for the promised signal, and neither of them left the terrace that day; but, however, they were disappointed, for it appeared not to their weary eyes.

Sad and comfortless they returned in the evening to their chamber, and passed the night in melancholy ruminations. From the short distance the Castello was from Venice, they conceived that Carlo would reach it in little more than three days; and, as it was likely that when he had explained his mission, a party of the holy brotherhood would be immediately sent with him by water, they would take still less time. At one moment they feared that Carlo had fallen a victim to the desperate undertaking; and at another, they imagined, that, delighted at having regained his liberty, he had forgot to perform his promise.

Thus passed the night, and now the morning sun broke in upon them, with his orient beams.

They ascended the terrace, and looked towards the appointed

place; but the mists still hung on the mountain tops, and made it impossible to discern any object.

Soon, however, the powerful rays of the sun dispersed the vapours of the night; and Antoni and De Clifford beheld, to their indescribable joy, a white pennant waving in the air, from the rugged summit of a lofty rock.

Antoni immediately answered the signal, which was then withdrawn; and returned with De Clifford, to consult on the way in which they could effect the entrance of the troops into the castle.

There was not any difficulty, with respect to the iron chair, as no men were ever kept in that part of the Castle; for when the horn was winded at the grate, two of the men were dispatched from that place, to let down the chair; this Antoni and De Clifford could themselves do; but how to open the grate, was an undertaking of a difficult nature.

At length Antoni, fruitful in resources, hit on the following plan.

Having sent for Bernardo, he informed him, that it being his natal day, he wished a double allowance of wine to be given to the banditti; and desired, that as two of them would be sufficient to watch at the grate, the other four might be allowed to join their comrades, to partake of the enlivening flask, adding, that there being no appearance of the brigantine's approach, no danger could occur.

The scheme succeeded to his utmost wishes, the wine was given out to the banditti, the four men were allowed to join their comrades, and soon the hall in which they were, became a scene of revelry and confusion.

Antoni, as if by mistake, sent twice the quantity of wine to the two men who were left to watch at the post where the iron wheel was that opened the grate below, and now impatiently waited until it was dark.

As soon as the nocturnal gloom thickened around, Antoni, accompanied by De Clifford, with palpitating hearts proceeded to the wheel: when they entered the place, the first object that they beheld was the two men laying on the floor, in a state of intoxication; and were pleased at seeing this, since they could effect their design without shedding their blood.

They immediately confined their legs and arms; and then exerting their strength, turned the wheel slowly, as creaked the grate below on its massy hinges; and, delighted with the success they had hitherto met with, they departed from the place, leaving the grate open, and proceeded to the tube in which was the iron chair; here they waited, anxiously listening if any sound should arise from the dark profundity.

At length a confused murmur of voices ascended from below, and struck on their delighted ears; instantly they lowered the chair, and when with some labour they had drawn it up again, they beheld the faithful Carlo, with two officers of the holy brotherhood.

The chair was again quickly lowered, and three of the soldiers were drawn up, and these now assisted to bring up the rest of the party.

Antoni embraced Carlo with much delight; and as soon as all the men were in the corridor, conducted them into the octagon hall.

That part of the Castello in which the banditti lived was now buried in profound silence; Antoni, anxious to see his beloved Laura, repaired instantly with some men to the chamber where Bernardo slept: they easily seized and confined him; and taking the keys from his girdle, with a beating heart Antoni conducted the soldiers through the passage beneath the black marble statue, to the hall where the banditti were.

These became an easy prey, being for the most part insensible of their situation, through the liquor they had drank, which had entirely overpowered their faculties. Those being confined, Antoni went to the dungeons, and having opened them, found many miserable captives, whom he released; but no where could he discover that one in which his Laura was confined.

Mad with the delay, he went back to the room where Bernardo was; but the barbarous wretch no sooner heard what he wanted, than grinning horribly at him, "No," said he, "the only consolation I have, the only way I can be revenged of you is, by letting the secret of the place she is confined in perish with me; and her death, which will soon happen when she is deprived of nourishment, will be a consolation to me in my last moments."

The commander of the party, enraged at his cruel designs, now ordered his men to torture him until he confessed.

Bernardo was soon dragged into the octagon hall, where the rope was which had so lately been made use of to torture the unhappy De Clifford: the loops were immediately placed round his arms, and the weights affixed to his legs, and he was drawn up in the air; the great strength of his body, however, enabled him to bear the weights without any great pain.

Seeing this, the officer ordered them to be doubled: Bernardo was now let down with a sudden jirk; the great pain occasioned by it produced a short groan.

He was now once more ordered to confess the place of Laura's confinement; but he refusing to answer, the additional weights were applied, and he was again drawn up.

The ropes under his arms now cut through the flesh, and the blood trickled down his sides, and the weight of the irons that were fastened to his feet, drew his legs out of their joints: unable to bear the agony, he groaned aloud, and the distortion of his features shewed how much he suffered.

The officer now again demanded if he would confess? for some time he was silent, and at length, on the question being put again to him, he faintly replied, "No, never while life remains."

Enraged at his obstinacy, the commander ordered him to be taken down, and to have his legs and arms broken.

Bernardo was now laid on a table, and one of the soldiers was lifting up the iron bar which was to break his limbs, when, fright-ened at the dreadful agony he was about to suffer, he motioned to the officer to approach; and then told him that he would point out the way to Signora Laura's chamber.

Antoni now had a plank brought, on which the suffering wretch was laid, and they proceeded down the stairs, and through the several passages to the dungeons.

The acute agony which had been caused by the tortures he had suffered, now made Bernardo for a time perfectly insensible; and Antoni wandered about the dreary passages, distracted with fear, lest Bernardo should die, before he had disclosed the secret entrance to the chamber where his adored Laura was.

At length signs of returning animation were perceived in Bernardo; and some wine being poured down his throat, he began slowly to revive: at length he motioned to the men who bore him to proceed; and as they carried him past the dungeon where De Clifford had been confined, he pointed to a large stone that was sunk in the ground.

In this stone was an iron ring, by which the men lifted it up, when a small flight of stairs appeared.

"The passage that those stairs lead to," said Bernardo, with difficulty, "is made in the walls of the Castello, and will bring you up its steep ascent to a door; in a niche in the wall you will perceive a key which belongs to it: as soon as you have opened it, proceed to the right, and the first door you then will come to is the Signora's chamber, of which you have got the key."

Having received these directions, Antoni flew down the steps, and then began to ascend the steep passage; De Clifford accompanied him with a torch. When they had toiled up the long corridor, they beheld a large door, and in the niche of the wall found a key; this he applied to the rusty wards of the lock, and at length heard the bolt retreat from the stone-work which encased the portal.

The door slowly creaking on its hinges, discovered to them several passages; taking the right, as directed by Bernardo, the agitated Antoni stopped at the first door, and began to try the several keys he held, to find out which was the right one: at length he was successful, and pushing open the door, entered the apartment, where he saw, and instantly held in his arms, his adored Laura.

The weak pen is inadequate to describe the meeting; and leaving the happy pair to their mutual congratulations, we will close this chapter, and relate the journey of Carlo, which so fortunately succeeded to the utmost extent of the wishes of Antoni and De Clifford.

CHAPTER XIV.

"He trod the water;
——————And breasted
The surge that met him: his bold head
'Bove the contentious waves he kept, and oar'd
Himself, with his good arms, in lusty stroke,
To the shore, that o'er his wave-worn basis bow'd,
As stooping to relieve him."

SHAKESPEARE.

WHEN Carlo was lowered down in the iron chair through the tube, by Antoni and De Clifford, he took with him a plank, by the assistance of which he was to support himself, while crossing the large sheet of water, which he must pass, before he entered the cavern where the iron grate was.

It was with infinite labour and perseverance that he accomplished this; but what was his horror, as he approached the grate, to hear it close.

For a long time he sat on his plank in a stupor of grief; at length recovering himself, in some degree, he proceeded to examine it, in the hope of finding some mode by which he might pass it.

He found it consisted of large bars of iron, closely placed together, fixed in stone-work beneath the water, and also in the rocky roof above the grate, which was broad and low, and only calculated to let one boat pass through at a time: the massy chains which prevented it from being opened, were drawn up through the rock above, and refused to move to his exertions.

Fatigued, desponding, and oppressed with grief, he rested himself on his plank, thinking that now he must either perish with want, as it was impossible for him to return back to the Castello, or else be found by Sebastiano when he returned, when he too well knew what would be his fate; and in which, it was not unlikely, both Antoni and De Clifford would be involved, since it must appear that two must be concerned in his escape, as less could not manage to raise up the chair.

It would be impossible to attempt to describe his sensations during the night: the pleasing ideas he had painted to himself, of shewing his gratitude to Antoni, and of again seeing his beloved Annetta, all vanished; and the vacuum was filled up with agonizing reflections on his unhappy situation, and his too certain destiny.

So passed the night in miserable ruminations; and the morning's dawn found poor Carlo seated on his plank, near the grate; frequently he raised his despairing eyes to look at it, and as often hopelessly withdrew them.

He now determined to go round the rocks which enclosed the sheet of water, to endeavour to find some passage by which he might gain their lofty summits; when, as he was preparing to depart, he heard the heavy chain clank, and looking up, saw it slowly descend; another chair that was under the water was now drawn up, and the grate slowly opened.

Transported with joy, Carlo instantly passed it, and proceeded on his way, free from the bars, chains, and massy fastenings of Strombolo.

His difficulties, however, ended not here; he had a great extent of the cavern still to pass; hope, however, urged him on, and he soon found himself borne on the rough waves of the Mediterranean.

His frame, exhausted by the fatigues it had undergone, could

ill cope with their force, and it was with the greatest difficulty
he preserved his frame from being dashed to pieces on the rough
and craggy rocks.

At length he espied a flat shelving rock, on which he gladly
got, and ascending up the craggy steps, soon found himself in a
place of security, and where he might repose his wearied limbs.
Fatigued by the great exertions and agitations he had undergone,
he resigned himself to the powerful arms of sleep.

Thus, had it not fortunately occurred to Antoni that there
was a possibility that Carlo might not have arrived at the grate
at the time he caused it to be drawn back, and in consequence
of that idea had had it opened the next morning, all his schemes
would have failed, and the poor Carlo, and probably himself and
De Clifford, would have fallen victims to the relentless fury of
Sebastiano.

Thus does an all-wise Providence prosper the designs of the
virtuous, and in his own appointed time, bring about the means
of their deliverance from their troubles; and, on the guilty authors
of their misery, finally pours down an ample vengeance for their
atrocious acts.

When Carlo awoke, he immediately pursued his way over the
lofty rocks, and at length descended from their rugged summits,
to the luxuriant vales below, directing his course for Venice, at
which place he was to make application for the forces of the
State, to seize the Castle De Strombolo.

Being strengthened by the sleep he had taken when he landed,
he pursued his way, only stopping to refresh himself at a peasant's cottage, and travelled the whole of that night.

The estate on which he had resided with his Annetta was but
a few leagues out of his road, and Carlo bent his way towards
it, to hear news of his family, from whom he had been forced,
by a party of Sebastiano's people, who beheld in the muscular
form of Carlo, a proper object to encrease the number of the
banditti.

In order to make up for the time he would lose by this deviation, he scarcely stopped to take the necessary refreshments, but pursued his way with all possible celerity.

He now, towards the evening, arrived in sight of the humble cottage where he had passed many a happy day with his family, and, with a beating heart, lifted up the latch of the lowly door; and entering into the room, saw his dear Annetta, who, at the unexpected sight, fell senseless on the floor.

Carlo, however, soon recovered her, and then related what had happened to him since their separation, and the business that now had happily given him an opportunity of escaping from the Castello.

Annetta, in return, related her tale, which contained little else than a recital of her grief for his loss, and the difficulty with which she had supported herself and family, during his absence: she then took him by the hand, and, with a look of love and fondness, led him into the next room, where, on a lowly pallet, reposed his two children.

The delighted Carlo imprinted the kiss of love on their rosy lips; and, seeing the day begin to break, with a sigh informed Annetta that he must depart.

Annetta made use of all her little rhetoric, to persuade him to remain at home, at least for that day; but Carlo had too high a sense of the promise he had made to Antoni, and fondly embracing her, departed.

Annetta continued at the door of her little cottage, waving her hand till he was out of sight, and then returned with a lightened heart, to her domestic employ.

Carlo in the mean time pursued his journey; and when he had ascended a hill, from which he could discover his lowly hut, stopped to gaze on it, while the wan tear of love and affection rose in his eye, at the remembrance of the happiness he had enjoyed there, with his Annetta and children, and which, there was now a probability, he would again partake of.

Hastily wiping away the moisture of sensibility, he continued his route; and taking that night a few hours repose, he beheld, when the bright beams of the morning sun had chased away the overhanging vapours of the night, the distant spires and steeples of the Venetian capital.

As soon as he arrived in that city, he went to the senate-house, where he requested to be heard, and having obtained permission, acquainted the senators with the abode of the banditti, and of the means by which they might be secured; adding, that Signor Antoni, who had been forced to accept of the situation of the second in command, would cause the troops of the State to be admitted.

A venerable senator now rose up, with great agitation in his countenance, and demanded of Carlo, if Signor Antoni bore no other name?

"His other name, Signor," said Carlo, "is Rhinaldo, but he is generally called, by the inhabitants of Strombolo, only Signor Antoni."

"Merciful powers!" exclaimed the old man, "it is my son, my much lamented Antoni, who was taken by an Italian pirate some years back. But why do I delay? I will this moment to the Doge, and request the troops of the holy brotherhood may be instantly dispatched to the place: meanwhile, do you, my friend," said he to Carlo, "go to my house, where every attention shall be paid to you, as becomes the deliverer of my son." Saying this, he instantly left the hall; and soon a party of men were in readiness to accompany Carlo.

The party now embarked on board some boats, and in two days anchored in a small bay, near the rocks which concealed the Castello De Strombolo.

Here Carlo went on shore towards the evening; but when he arrived at the appointed place, it was too dark for his signal to be perceived: impatiently he waited till the morning's dawn, when he had the satisfaction to find it answered. He therefore hastily returned to the party, and having acquainted the officer who commanded, with the disposition which had been made by Antoni, of admitting the troops into the Castello at midnight, he ordered the party to be in readiness, as soon as the shades of night descended on the earth; and then permitted the men to go on shore, to refresh themselves after their confinement.

When the sun began to sink in the western ocean, the party embarked, and, directed by Carlo, proceeded through the caverns, and passed the grate, which was open; they then crossed the broad sheet of water, and at length landed on the stone pavement, which was under the tube. They had not been long there when the iron chair descended, into which two of the officers and Carlo seated themselves, and were soon drawn up by Antoni and De Clifford.

Thus have we described the adventures of the trusty and faithful Carlo; and now we will proceed with the occurrences that took place in the Castello De Strombolo, which was now in the possession of the troops of the holy brotherhood.

CHAPTER XV.

"As meet two broad-winged eagles in their sounding strife, in winds, so rushed the chief to the fight."   OSSIAN.

"Gasping he lay, and from the grissly wound,
     The crimson life ebb'd out upon the ground."
                                             BLACKMORE.

"A gloomy night o'erwhelms his dying eyes,
     And his disdainful soul from his pale bosom flies."
                                             BLACKMORE.

THE officer who commanded the party in possession of Strombolo, fearful that should Sebastiano return, and find the grate open, and the boats which had been left in the cavern, near the tube, ordered them to be taken away to the small bay in which they had anchored, when Carlo left them to make the appointed signal.

He also had the grate closed, and appointed some of his men

to watch in the chamber above it, who were instructed in the signal they would receive from Sebastiano's people when they arrived.

Antoni, in the society and converse of his adored Laura, forgot all his former cares; and on the second evening, when they were sitting on the terrace, watching the declining sun, he requested she would inform him in what way she had been carried a prisoner into the Castello De Strombolo?

"My dear Antoni," said Laura, "I must first make you acquainted with a circumstance, which will immediately make clear to you, what at present seems a mystery. Sebastiano is no other than the wretch Rugantino, who, you know, twice unsuccessfully attempted to carry me off."

"Gracious Heaven! is it possible?" exclaimed Antoni; "it does indeed open my eyes to the whole dark transaction."

"When Sebastiano," continued Laura, "discovered that he had in his power the husband of her whom he wished to possess, and who had so completely baffled his well-drawn plans to get her in his power, he at first, as he has informed me, was resolved to destroy you; but, as you had saved his life; he felt himself unable to do it; he therefore contented himself with keeping you with him; and that he might have you more constantly under his eye, made you the second in command, which his men, who had witnessed your bravery, readily consented to. Now that you were safe, he thought he could the more easily put into force his plans for securing me, and which he but too well succeeded in. By a large sum of money he bribed my servants, and in the dead of night entered my chamber, and ordered me to rise: seeing that I hesitated, he wrapped the cloaths around me, and covering my head up in them, to prevent my screams being heard, in that situation, almost unable to breathe, I was put in a boat, and conveyed on board the brigantine; and soon after found myself in these horrid walls. Sebastiano now informed me of what I have just before related to you, and made proffers of his love to me, which I received with every mark of contempt and scorn.

When he found himself disappointed in his schemes, he abated in the frequency of his visits; and the horrid Bernardo was the only one who entered my chamber, and that but on certain days, for the purpose of bringing me provisions. When I first came to the Castello, Sebastiano sent a guitar to me, which he had found on board some vessel which had fallen into his power; and with this instrument I used to beguile the melancholy hours, in hopes that by some chance you might hear my voice. Bernardo, who had the charge of me, had strict orders never to let you visit the dungeons; and it was owing to that precaution that you remained in ignorance of my situation."

A distant horn was now heard to wind; and Antoni and De Clifford, starting up, ran to acquaint the commander of the troops with the arrival of Sebastiano and his party, who were now at the grate. Antoni then returned, and conducted the trembling agitated Laura to a place of safety; and then arming himself, joined the troops.

Agreeable to his advice, the party secreted themselves in the chambers that surrounded the octagon hall; from whence it was settled that they should rush out, on a given signal, when Sebastiano and his party had arrived in it; who would then be easily secured, when so unexpectedly surprised.

Some of the men who had been forced into the service of Sebastiano, were ordered to attend to the iron chair, whither they immediately went, and at the well-known horn lowered it.

Sebastiano and his party were soon admitted, and proceeded directly to the octagon hall. As soon as they entered it, the portal was closed, and this was the signal for the troops, who instantly threw open the doors which concealed them, and appeared, with the officer at their head, who ordered them instantly to lay down their arms, or be cut to pieces.

Amazement for a moment occupied each of the banditti, till Sebastiano, drawing his sword, rushed furiously on them, crying out to his men to follow him.

The banditti, who were all armed, instantly pursued his example, and a dreadful carnage ensued.

In the heat of the engagement, Antoni and Sebastiano were opposed to each other; when Sebastiano, with a deadly curse, aimed a furious blow at him, saying, "This to thy heart, traitor."

Antoni easily avoided the intended thrust, and taking advantage of the intemperate rage of Sebastiano, as he was recovering himself, pierced his body, saying, "This for Laura's wrongs."

Deluged in his blood, Sebastiano fell; and the remainder of the party, seeing their leader vanquished, now sued for mercy.

As soon as those who remained alive were secured, and a guard placed over them, Antoni examined the body of Sebastiano, but the breath of life had ceased to animate his guilty form, and he lay extended a hideous corpse.

Antoni soon calmed the agitation of his Laura, by his presence; and now they prepared to leave the Castello. The commander of the troops gave them letters to the State, to inform them of the event of their operations, and stating the quantity of plunder that there was in the Castle; for the doors that were in the passage, which led to Laura's apartment, led to the cave where Sebastiano kept his ill-got treasures, and which place was only known to him and Bernardo.

On the second morning Antoni and his Laura, accompanied by De Clifford, and the delighted Carlo, were lowered down, with some of the other unfortunate prisoners, who had been long detained in the frowning walls of Strombolo; and embarking in the boat which had brought Sebastiano and his people, they proceeded, for the last time, through the gloomy caverns and strong grate, and soon arrived at Venice.

The people, who had been apprised of their arrival, ran in crowds to see them; and Antoni and Laura soon found themselves in the arms of their delighted parents.

De Clifford for some time resided with Antoni; and at length conceiving his presence would be necessary in England, he determined to repair there; and accordingly wrote to acquaint

Father Oswald, whom he had left at his Castle, of his intention, at the same time giving him an account of the misfortune he had met with, in being taken by Sebastiano.

Carlo was enabled, by the munificence of the grateful Antoni, to pass the remainder of his days, with his Annetta and children, in a comfortable independence.

Bernardo, with some of the principal ferocious wretches, that composed the banditti, were brought to Venice, where they were tried by the justly-incensed laws of their country; and were sentenced to be broke on the wheel, and the rest were confined to the gallies for life.

The morning being arrived which was fixed for their execution, an immense concourse of spectators flocked round the scaffold, on which they were to terminate their guilty existence, when the gigantic form of Bernardo underwent the punishment it had so richly deserved, and soon became a motionless corpse.

The others were now brought forward to suffer the same fate, and died in full conviction that their punishment was their just desert.

The treasures that were found in the Castello De Strombolo were confiscated, and the lofty walls, which rose in stern defiance to the consuming hand of Time, were razed to the ground.

Signor Antoni Rhinaldo, and his beautiful Laura, now that the savage enemy of their repose was no more, enjoyed uninterrupted quiet; and De Clifford, who beheld their domestic happiness, sighed to think that such would have been his portion, had not the unrelenting fates cut short the thread of his beauteous Matilda's existence.

He soon became restless and unquiet, and refusing to hearken to the solicitations of Antoni, to make his habitation his residence, till the lenient hand of Time had blunted the edge of his grief, procured a passage in a ship which was soon to steer its course for England.

Many delays, however, hindered the vessel from being ready for her voyage; but at length her hollow sides were stored with the valuable merchandize of the Mediterranean ports; and De Clifford, taking leave of Antoni and his Laura, embarked on board of the bark.

Prosperous gales winged them on through the wide world of waters, and the distant shores of Italy appeared only as a cloud in the horizon, till at length they faded from the view.

Now they passed by the Spanish coast, and again saw the lofty Rock of Gibraltar, rearing its rugged summit amid the overhanging clouds, which the Levant winds bear on their broad pinions.

The rolling waves of the Bay of Biscay now agitated the bark, and soon were perceived the lofty shores of Albion, which the glad mariners hailed with delight; and soon cast their crooked anchor in the yellow sands of the spacious Bay of Tor, so called from the lofty hills which form its sides.

CHAPTER XVI.

"Canst thou not minister to a mind diseas'd,
Pluck from the memory a rooted sorrow,
Raze out the written troubles of the brain;
And with some sweet oblivious antidote,
Cleanse the stuff'd bosom of that perilous stuff,
That weighs upon the heart?"

SHAKESPEARE.

"Oh my soul's joy,
If after we'ry tempest come sweet calm,
May the winds blow 'till they have waken'd death."

SHAKESPEARE.

As soon as De Clifford landed, he went to his Castle, where he was received, with the greatest joy, by Father Oswald, and his domestics, who, being apprized of his return by the venerable Father, who had received the letter which De Clifford sent him from Venice, advanced on the road to meet him, as soon as they heard he was coming, with acclamations of joy and gladness.

De Clifford embraced his venerable friend, the Father, with real pleasure, and received the welcome of his delighted vassals, with unfeigned satisfaction.

Still, however, his mind was a prey to melancholy; and Matilda—the lovely fascinating Matilda—now, alas! no more, occupied his thoughts; and Father Oswald saw that the grief he indulged had taken too deep root ever to be extirpated, and that his travels had not been of any service to him.

Father Oswald, in answer to his enquiries about the inhabitants of Berry Pomeroy Castle, informed him, that since he had been absent, the Lady Elinor was married to Sir Ethelred De Fortebrand, who had died suddenly, but a few weeks back:—he also informed him of the advancement, through the medium of Lady Elinor, of Father Bertrand to the Abbotship of Ford Abbey; and that since he had obtained that situation, he no longer wore the mask of dissimulation, but governed the venerable Fathers of the Monastery with such haughty authority, that to many of them, especially those who did not agree to his arbitrary measures, their existence was become a burthen, which even religion could scarcely ease the weight of; some of them had left the place, and sought repose in other places dedicated to devotion, where the superiors were men of piety and learning.

Father Oswald added, that whatever was the conduct of the Abbot Bertrand towards the monks, his deportment to the Lady Elinor, his patroness, was submissive and respectful in the highest degree; and seldom a day passed, without his being at the Castle of Berry Pomeroy.

De Clifford listened to this recital with some surprise, that such eventful occurrences could have taken place in the short time he was absent, and which scarcely exceeded a year, in which time the Lady Elinor had married, and was now a widow.

While engaged in these thoughts, the idea rose to his mind of again revisiting the tomb of the sainted Matilda—now, he supposed, neglected and forgot by all but him, who cherished her fond remembrance in his heart, and felt displeased, when any accidental occurrence made him, for a moment, forget her.

He did not disclose his intentions to Father Oswald, who might, doubtless, argue against such an indulgence of useless grief, and whose encreasing infirmities would make it dangerous for him to encounter the midnight air; for it was at that time only that De Clifford could indulge his sorrows, at the tomb of his adored Matilda, uninterrupted by the prying eye of curiosity.

He desired the faithful Hubert, whose grief at the supposed loss of his master in the engagement with Sebastiano's brigantine had been increasing, and whose delight, when informed by Father Oswald that he had received intelligence of his not only being alive, but on the point of returning to his estate, was beyond all bounds, to endeavour to procure the key of the subterraneous passage, which led to the chapel of the Castle of Berry Pomeroy, by some means, from the castellain, in whose possession it was.

The task appeared a difficult one; however, Hubert cheerfully undertook it; and De Clifford, that he might afford him a pretence for visiting the Castle, sent by him a consolatory message to the now Lady Elinor De Fortebrand, on the death of Sir Ethelred.

Hubert soon arrived at the Castle, and, delivering his message, was desired to wait in the hall, until the Lady Elinor should be acquainted with it. He had not been long there, when she herself appeared, clad in flowing robes of sable.

She accosted him with great kindness and affability, and having received his message from himself, returned a suitable answer; and then sending the chief officer of her household, charged him to make welcome the domestic of Sir Henry De Clifford. The man bowed obedience, and the Lady Elinor retired from the hall.

The castellain, who had been commissioned to treat Hubert with attention, conducted him to his apartment, where he invited him to partake of the enlivening flask.

Hubert, as he entered, saw with pleasure that the room he was in was that where the keys of the Castle were kept: these were all hung up against the walls, with labels, denoting to what portals or gates they belonged.

Hubert was determined to endeavour to procure the key himself, privately, as his asking for it might create suspicion, and a refusal.

As the door, of which he wished to obtain the key, was on the south side, he directed his eyes, when unperceived by the castellain, to that part of the chamber; and at length perceived, in the corner, a small key, on the label of which he could distinguish the word "vaults;" this therefore, he concluded, must be the object of his search; and watching an opportunity, when the castellain left the chamber to fetch another flask of wine from the Castle stores, he arose, and, taking the key down, concealed it in his doublet.

Pleased with having so easily obtained the object of his mission, he staid to empty, with the castellain, the second flask; and then bent his steps towards De Clifford Castle, and, with much satisfaction, delivered the key to his master.

De Clifford determined to go the next evening, to pass his lonely hours, in indulging his griefs, at the shrine of the beloved, revered, object of his soul's affections; and when that time arrived, and the shades of night condensed on the earth, taking a lamp in his hand, he left his Castle, by a private postern, and proceeded towards Berry Pomeroy Castle.

He soon arrived at the well-known valley, over whose green fields rises the proud turrets of the Castle; and, for a moment, stood wrapt in contemplation, at the beauty of the scene which presented itself to him.

The moon, which shone in full beauty, threw her silver beams over the various foliage of the trees, that hung on the romantic steeps which surrounded the valley, and glittered in the moving bosom of the clear sheet of water; the grey walls of the Castle were illumined by her mild radiance, and formed altogether so pleasing, so beautiful a picture, as would make fruitless the endeavours of the most able artist to imitate.

De Clifford now ascended the winding path which led to the Castle; and sighed, to think how often he had impatiently traced it, to enjoy the sweet converse of her to whose tomb he was now proceeding—a sorrowing, miserable, isolated being, without one gleam of hope or comfort, to soothe the sad remainder of his days!

How oft, too, had he walked here with her—had seen her intelligent countenance beam with delight, while surveying the different beauties of the prospect, as they presented themselves to the pleased sight!

Those eyes that sparkled with animation, now sealed up by the hand of death—those downy cheeks, the abode of the blushing rose, now pale, and cold—and that form, whose airy elegance dwelt on his ravished view, now inanimate, and consigned to the solitary tomb!—and himself left a wanderer on the earth—and the link, that made it appear a blissful abode, broken asunder for ever!

De Clifford, amidst these harrowing reflections, arrived at the walls of the Castle, and soon found out the small door that led to the chapel; this he opened, and was on the point of uncovering the lamp he held, to illuminate the dusky interior, when he thought he saw, as he looked into the passage, a light, at the further end; he immediately entered it, and closed the door behind him, that the light of the moon might not discover him—and distinctly perceived a tall figure glide along, bearing a lamp.

At first he was fearful that the person, whoever it was, was approaching the door he had entered; but shortly after, he saw the mysterious figure turn into another passage; and soon the sound of its footsteps became indistinct.

De Clifford waited some time, that the person might be far enough away for him to advance, without fear of being discovered; and at length he uncovered his lamp, and began cautiously to proceed through the passage—when he again heard footsteps approaching; and, hastily covering his lamp, stood concealed behind a large rough column that supported the roof.

The figure now approached very near where he stood: it was that of a tall man, whose face was completely hid in his garments.

It appeared that this nightly wanderer had come for some secret purpose, into those subterraneous passages; and, that having performed the object he had in view, was returning.

De Clifford watched the figure till it disappeared; and then proceeded towards the tomb of his Matilda.

A solemn silence pervaded the chapel; the moon threw her bright beams through the lofty casements over the altar, and shone full on the marble monument of her whom he so sincerely adored.

De Clifford threw himself on his knees before it; "Pure angel," said he, "whose lifeless form this tomb contains, look down from thy bright abode, on thy still sorrowing, still miserable De Clifford, whose hapless fate it is to drag on life's weary burthen!"

He now hid his face in his hands—and for some time his grief denied his further utterance—when a soft voice, in well-known accents, said, "De Clifford, be comforted!"

"Merciful Heaven!" said De Clifford, starting up, "'tis her voice which I heard! O where art thou, fair angel?" said he, and wildly gazing around, perceived a female form, retreating through the dusky aisle.

De Clifford instantly flew after it; the form redoubled its pace—at length it sunk on the marble pavement; and De Clifford, seizing it in his arms, found he held not a cold breathless corpse, but the wan, palpitating, agitated form of his adored Matilda!

CHAPTER XVII.

"A sleep, dull as your last, did you arrest,
And all the magazines of life possess'd;
No more the blood its circling course did run,
But in the veins like isicles it hung:
No more the heart, now void of quick'ning heat,
The tuneful march of vital motion beat;
Stiffness did into all the sinews climb,
And a short death crept cold through ev'ry limb."

OLDHAM.

FATHER BERTRAND, when the Lady Elinor threw out her dark
hints concerning her sister, the Lady Matilda, formed instantly,
in his fertile mind, a plan, by which he would at all times retain
an ascendancy over her, should it be necessary, for any fulfilment
of his purposes.

He was, as we have before observed, skilled in herbal knowledge; when, therefore, he found the Lady Elinor bent on the
destruction of her sister, he seemed to acquiesce in her dark
design; and accordingly prepared a potion for her to give to her
unconscious victim, which possessed the quality of inflicting
grievous pains to the taker, but which at last acted on the
harrassed frame, as a powerful soporific, giving for a while, on
the distorted features, the appearance of death.

How well he succeeded has been related; and when he found
that the Lady Matilda was mourned for as a departed saint, he
became anxious that she should be quickly laid in the silent tomb,
when he would put the remainder of his plans into execution.

From the time he had given the potent liquor to the Lady
Elinor, he sought, with much anxiety, for a place fitting to convey
the Lady Matilda to, when she should awake from her deathlike
slumber.

In traversing the extensive vaults and subterraneous passages, which nature and art had formed, under the lofty towers of Berry Pomeroy Castle, Bertrand found a place exactly suited to his purposes, and which seemed to have been made for the concealment of some person.

At the termination of a long passage was a small chamber, which received light from a grating above; in the corner of this chamber he discovered a trap-door, which he raised; and seeing a ladder made of ropes attached to the sides of the aperture, he descended, by its assistance, into the place below, which he found to be a similar room to that above.

A grating in the wall, covered by a casement, admitted the light of the sun through the thick leafy branches of the trees that overhung it; a bed, a table, and a chair, all in a decayed state, constituted the furniture.

Bertrand viewed the place with much satisfaction—it was precisely what he wished for; and, without delay, he changed the present dilapidated furniture, for some which he secretly conveyed from the interior chambers of the Castle.

He next examined in what side of the Castle it was situated; and, with some difficulty, discovered by the grating, that it was made in the side of the steep declivity which was covered to the vale below, with thick grown trees, and appeared to defy all search.

As soon as the interment of the Lady Matilda was completed, he left the Castle, but, by a private postern, of which he had obtained the key, he entered directly the subterraneous vaults, pursued his way to the chapel, and opening the monument, took from the coffin the passive form of the Lady Matilda, and bore it to the chamber below, where he laid it on the couch.

He then quickly returned, and closing the monument, unbarred the portals of the chapel, which he had taken the precaution to fasten, lest any of the inhabitants of the Castle, impelled by curiosity to see the tomb of Matilda, or religious motives, might visit it, and discover his operations.

Having so far succeeded, he retraced his way back to the

secret chamber, and seating himself by the side of the couch, on which lay the hapless Matilda, awaited with much anxiety, until returning life should animate her features.

In a few hours a faint pulsation was perceptible, and Bertrand now essayed to raise her up, and put into her mouth a reviving cordial.

When Matilda opened her eyes, for some time she fixed them on the monk, and said, in a low trembling voice, "Is not that Father Bertrand I see?—where am I? where is De Clifford, who but now I was with? where is Father Oswald and my sister?"

"They are all well, Lady," said the Monk; "I pray you compose your spirits."

"Good heavens! where am I?" said the Lady Matilda; and raising herself up on her couch, and looking wildly around—"tell me, Father, I conjure you, lest my brain madden with apprehension."

"In my power," said the savage Bertrand, regarding her with a ferocious aspect:—"Nay, you may look round you—this is your prison. Your sister designed to deprive you of life; I have saved it—and now this must be your residence."

Here the Monk stopped, and rising up, paced the chamber; at times regarding her with a look that denoted he was deaf to the calls of pity or compassion.

Matilda turned away from his dark lowering features, and began to reflect on her situation: she now recollected the dark threats of her sister, when she found herself neglected in the will of Sir Hugh, her father; and she concluded that she had contrived, through the medium of the Monk, to confine her in that solitary dungeon, that she might enjoy the uncontrouled possession of the rich domains of Berry Pomeroy; and that in that melancholy abode, she was to pass the remainder of her days.

Overcome with ideas of so horrible a nature, her senses forsook her, and she sunk back on her couch, and remained for a while insensible to the horrors of her situation.

When she opened her eyes, the Monk was sitting by the side of the couch, and seemed to be involved in a deep rumination: as soon, however, as he saw that the Lady Matilda moved, and that life again had returned, he arose from his chair, and leaning over the couch, drew a dagger from his vestments, which he directed to the trembling bosom of Matilda; and presenting a small crucifix to her, said, in a hollow voice—

"Swear, Lady, by Him, whose image thou now beholdest, that thou wilt never make known thy existence to any one, whilst I exist; or this dagger instantly enters your heart."

"To what purpose is such an oath?" replied the trembling Matilda—"am I not safe here in your power?"

"Swear," said the Monk, in a louder voice, "or I will soon render myself secure by your death."

This said, he raised the dagger; and the hapless Matilda, who saw its sharp point ready to deprive her of existence, still clung to life; and putting the crucifix to her lips, said in a faint voice—"I swear—"

"Enough," said the Monk, withdrawing the dagger; "relying on thy oath, thou shalt enjoy many comforts, which else thou couldest not. I must now leave thee, Lady, for the shades of night are descending, and I must provide thee somewhat of provision, to refresh thy exhausted frame." So saying, he departed the chamber by the tackled stair.

Matilda, when he had departed, essayed to rise from her couch, and with difficulty, owing to the weak trembling state of her body, effected it: she approached the casement, and sought to discover where she was, but the gloom of evening enveloped the objects seen through the pendant branches of the surrounding trees, in dim obscurity: sighing, she thought of her oath, which was irrecoverable, and which could not be broken.

She gazed around on the walls of her chamber with a melancholy scrutiny:—"And ye," said she, "are to be the witnesses to my dreary existence. O, De Clifford, well do I recollect thy speechless agonies, when thou thoughtest that I was leaving this vale of misery: what would now be thy rage, didst thou know my situation; but that, alas! I have sworn to keep a secret, and thou must never know it."

Her habiliments now caught her eye; they were those of the grave—"Good heavens!" said she, "is it possible? have I then been committed to the silent tomb, during my insensibility, and plucked from forth its marble jaws, and conveyed here? It must be so indeed."

As several articles of dress had before attracted her notice, which were laying in a heap near the bed, she advanced to them; and on examination found them to be her own; and impatiently she divested herself of her melancholy apparel, and put on others more suitable.

The gloomy obscurity of her chamber now so much increased, that soon the objects within became imperceptible; and the dejected bewildered Matilda seated herself on a chair, awaiting the promised return of the Monk.

At length she heard his steps, as they sounded along the arched vaults and passages above, and perceived the rays of the lamp he held, descend through the trap-door; in the roof he soon appeared, bringing with him a basket.

He soon remarked that Matilda had changed her dress, which seemed to please him; and he now set before her some provisions, of which, exhausted as she was for want of their reviving aid, she gladly partook.

When she had concluded her repast, she demanded of the Monk, in what place she was in?

"You are now, Lady," said Bertrand, "in the vaults of your own Castle; by ascending that ladder, you will get into a chamber above, the door of which is to be opened by a secret spring, which appears to the observer as the head of a nail; when you touch this, the door, released from its bonds, will open, and you then are in a long passage; through this you pass, and at the upper end turn to the right; when soon before you will appear a flight of steps; these lead to the Castle chapel: I shall, trusting to your oath,

Lady, give you permission to walk about there, in the silent hour of midnight, when the Castle is buried in slumber; but recollect your oath—and that the smallest deviation from it will be your death. I shall leave you now, Lady, but every third night you may expect me with your provisions: I have also brought you oil for your lamp, that when the shades of night descend, you may illumine your apartment."

So saying, he departed and left the miserable and dejected Matilda, to her own sad thoughts and ruminations.

CHAPTER XVIII.

————"All days
Henceforth are equal;
To-morrow, and the next, and each that follows,
Will undistinguish'd roll, and but prolong
Once hated line of more extended woe."

CONGREVE.

THE bright beams of the morning beheld the hapless Matilda, seated by the small casement, pale, dejected and melancholy: the remembrance of the vow she had taken not to make her situation known, and which neither her honour nor her conscience permitted her to break, dwelt heavily on her mind.

She was fated no more to behold De Clifford, whom she adored with all the ardour of the fondest affection, but to pass her unhappy days amidst the gloomy caverns of her own Castle.

Thus passed the first day of Matilda's captivity; and soon as the evening shades descended on the earth, she lit her lamp, and waited till she imagined the inhabitants of the Castle would have retired for the night, that she might enter the chapel, and pay her devotions at the altar, and to implore the assistance of the saints, to support her in her cruel afflictions.

Bertrand, who knew sufficiently of the character and disposition of Matilda, to satisfy him of her strict observance of any solemn promise she might enter into, and who, for many reasons, wished not to make her confinement too severe; for he rather wished to be considered as a friend to her, in thus preserving her from the fell intents of her merciless sister, than to act from any views of his own; and knowing, that if such were her ideas, she would not fail to reward him, should he ever find it necessary to produce her to the world; and which, should the Lady Elinor fail in the performance of her promise, of making him the Superior of Ford, on the demise of the present abbot, he undoubtedly meant to do—did not hesitate to give her permission to leave her chamber; or indeed to do any thing she chose, which would not lead to a discovery; hoping, by such steps, to gain her confidence and interest, should she, once more, by his means, have possession of her estates.

Matilda, ascending the stairs, entered the upper chamber, and advanced to the door, at the side of which she discovered the small projection of iron, which the Monk had informed her of; this she pressed, and immediately the door gently opened.

Holding up her lamp, to throw its rays further into the gloomy passage that now appeared to her, Matilda proceeded along the passage, the extent of which greatly surprised her.

When at length she had reached the end, she saw two passages, one on each side; taking the right one, according to the Monk's direction, she soon beheld the stairs; and ascending them, came into the chapel, where the first object that struck her view was the tomb in which she had been enclosed. Sighing, she viewed it; and almost wished that she had remained its inhabitant, free from the torturous sensations her present situation forced her to feel.

Setting down her lamp, she threw herself on her knees before the altar; and besought the Deity to give her fortitude, to bear up with her present calamity; she prayed also for the repose of De Clifford; and entreated heaven to forgive her guilty sister.

Rising off her knees, she felt her spirits more composed; and, casting her beauteous eyes up to heaven, with a grateful look, retired to her solitary chamber.

Thus passed the first two months of her dreary seclusion; when, one night, as she was walking about the chapel, she felt a great wish to see if her chambers were inhabited; for, if they were not, and she could enter them, she would possess herself of some manuscripts which were there, and which would serve to beguile the tedious hours.

With light and cautious steps she traversed the long corridors, and coming to the portal that opened into her suite of apartments, with joy beheld the key in the lock; slowly she opened the door; and looking around her, saw clearly, from the confused state the chamber was in, that it was uninhabited.

Taking courage from this idea, she drew the key out of the door—and entering the chamber, locked herself in, that she might, without fear of being disturbed, procure the books she wished to have.

Matilda passed on into the chamber, where was the couch, on which, it was supposed, she had departed this world of care and woe.

The ensignias of death had been left on it; a large velvet pall covered the whole of the bed, and the lofty tester was hung with black drapery.

Through this dismal apartment she entered a closet, which she was used to dedicate to devotional exercises: the crucifix and beads were on the table, and, by their side, a lute: this she took up, and touched its trembling stops; then by a sudden impulse, she drew from its varying notes the tune of her morning hymn: reflecting, however, that she might raise the curious observance of some wakeful person, she laid down the instrument, and commenced her search after the books—these having found, she retraced her steps to the outward portal of the chambers, and was just going to turn the key, when she heard some steps in the corridor.

Trembling, she desisted, and attentively listened to the sound: the echo of the steps now died away; and at last she cautiously opened the door, and not seeing any person, quickly sought her melancholy chamber; where she found that the Monk had been, during her absence, with her provisions.

In perusing the books she had brought with her, she passed her days; and regularly, at midnight, would she repair to the altar, to offer up her prayers to the Divine Being. One night as she was about to enter the chapel, she heard the moans of some person who was in it.—Setting her lamp beneath the winding staircase, she softly advanced into it, and the voice of De Clifford, calling on her to descend from the realms of light, and appear to his aching eyes, smote her astonished ear.

Taking pity on his hapless situation, she slowly advanced, and calling on him by name, spoke some few words of comfort, in an agitated voice; and then praying heaven to bless him, receded from his sight, and, with breathless agitation, hastened to her chamber.

Some days after, she was informed by Bertrand, who then had attained the elevated situation of Abbot, that De Clifford had left the kingdom. Matilda was unhappy at this intelligence; although she felt but too well assured of the insurmountable bar to the possession of him she adored, yet the idea that he was near her, afforded her a degree of content, which she was now unhappily deprived of.

But when, some time after, the Abbot informed her that he was no more—her spirits, ill able to bear so great and so severe a shock, sunk under the calamity; and for a time she daily expected to meet him in the blissful abodes above.

Her good constitution, however, and her resignation to the will of her Almighty Creator, enabled her to arise from her couch; and she soon resumed her accustomed walks about the Castle.

The first evening she went forth, she turned towards her apartments; and as she walked along the corridor, wrapt up in a melancholy reverie, she observed not that she had passed the portal of her late chambers; and continued on, when some words, which she heard spoke by a well-known voice, caused her to stop, and look around her, when she was surprised to find herself opposite to the suite of apartments which belonged to her sister, the Lady Elinor.

With much surprise, she now heard her sister's voice, calling on De Clifford, in the melancholy strain of a hopeless passion; and saying, that, but for him, she would still have been happy, still innocent of the death of her sister.

The tears streamed down the pale face of Matilda, as she heard Elinor calling on her to look down and pity her; and, actuated by a sudden impulse, she gently opened the door, and saw the melancholy form of her sister, sitting by the casement—the gloom which enveloped the room, and the sighs and faltering voice of Elinor, prevented her from observing her sister, or hearing her approach.

From the tenor of her discourse, Matilda concluded that the fate of De Clifford was as yet unknown to her: wishing, therefore, to acquaint her with his departure from this world of care, she first, in a slow voice, assured her of her pity and forgiveness; and then, in order that she might repent of her ill-passed life, she related, in a solemn tone, that the unhappy De Clifford was entombed in the unfathomed depths of the ocean, and that his blood rested on her, who had been so instrumental to his fate: then, conjuring her to repent, to think of an hereafter, and to prepare herself for it, she withdrew; and, as she was advancing to the door, she saw her sister, after uttering a loud scream, fall senseless on the floor.

Fearful of being discovered, Matilda darted out of the room, and, taking up her lamp, which she had left in the corridor, hurried along until she came to the chapel; then, pausing to take breath, and recover herself, she proceeded to her apartment; when, throwing her agitated form on the couch, she passed a sleepless night in unavailing sighs and tears, at the fate of the unfortunate De Clifford.

CHAPTER XIX.

"Who in the paths of virtue perseveres,
Has nought to apprehend from impious men."

E. HAYWOOD.

"Virtue may be assail'd, but never hurt;
Surpris'd, by unjust force, but not enthrall'd:
Yea, even that which mischief means most harm,
Shall, in the happy trial, prove most glory."

MILTON.

EARLY the next morning, Matilda heard some steps in the apartment above, and soon saw the Abbot descend—he approached her, with a dark and ferocious aspect, and, unsheathing a dagger, bid her prepare for death.

"You have," said he, in a hollow tone, "disobeyed my strict injunctions, and now shall suffer the destined punishment."

Saying this, he lifted up the instrument of death, with a threatening look, and prepared to plunge it into the heaving breast of Matilda; who, sinking down on her knees, besought him to have mercy on her; and then, in a faltering agitated voice, related every circumstance that had occurred; and, that moved with pity at the situation of her sister, and wishing to warn her to a speedy repentance, had addressed some few words to her; but that she was convinced that her sister thought that the visitation was a supernatural one; and that therefore she had not discovered herself, nor broke her promise made to him, and therefore entreated his compassion.

The Monk, during her discourse, slowly withdrew the sharp instrument of death, and, for a time, seemed to reflect; at length, looking on the prostrate Matilda—

"Rise, Lady," said he; "for this once I spare thy life; but remember, from this time, the apartment above is all the space

234

allowed thee; the portal of that chamber will, from henceforth, be fastened." So saying, he departed.

Matilda, rising up, sought to compose the agitation the savage Bertrand, by his threat, had thrown her in; and, raising her eyes to heaven, piously breathed forth a grateful prayer, for her escape from dissolution.—The being deprived of her liberty affected her much; and now her few books were her only consolation.

In this manner she passed many months; when one stormy night, as she lay on her couch, listening to the wind, as it howled among the surrounding forest, a sudden gust seemed to shake the wall, at the head of her bed.

Matilda, greatly surprised at this circumstance, determined, as soon as the morning dawned, to endeavour to find out the cause. As soon, therefore, as there was sufficient light for her design, she arose, and, with much difficulty, at last succeeded in removing the cumbrous couch; when, striking the wall, she found it sent forth a hollow sound, and a large pannel of the wainscot shook.

Matilda, convinced that this was a concealed door, examined around it with great attention, to find out its fastenings: for some time her search was fruitless; at last, however, she succeeded, and found out the spring which fastened it, when, pushing it aside, she entered another chamber, in which was a flight of steps; the height of which, owing to the surrounding gloom, she could not discover; and, fearful of venturing up them, lest they might open on some habited part of the Castle, and so risk the danger of discovering herself, she returned, closed the pannel, and then replaced the couch, so that she could, without the trouble of moving it again, have access to the pannel.

This employed her some time, and after she had compleated it, she felt herself much fatigued; and, having passed a sleepless night, owing to the continual howling of the winds, sought a few hours repose on her couch, to which she repaired; and soon were her eyes closed, and she enjoyed a short forgetfulness of her unhappy situation.

When she awoke, the sun had withdrawn his gladsome rays, and evening, in her russet mantle, enveloped the earth. Having illumined her apartment with the light of her lamp, she partook of her provisions; and, as soon as she deemed it safe, opened the pannel, and began to ascend the long flight of steps.

There she wound up a great height; and she was filled with surprise and wonder to find, by the loop-holes which she at times met, and looking through saw, that it was in the wall of the Southern turret that these stairs were formed.

When, with some labour and difficulty, she at length arrived at the summit, she beheld two doors, from one of which she removed the strong bars that fastened it; and opening it, a sudden blast nearly extinguished her lamp; hastily she closed it, and descending a few steps, set it down in a niche in the wall, and then again opened the door.

The cloudy sky, with a few twinkling stars, sometimes hid by the dark scud that swiftly passed along, now met her view; a few steps were before her, which she ascended, and found herself on the battlements of the turrets.

The cold nocturnal breeze chilled her weak frame, and she quickly returned back, and fastening the door, proceeded to loose the bars, and to draw back the bolts of the other portal, which, with long disuse, were rusted in the mortices; however, this she accomplished, and, pushing the door from her, it slowly gave way to her efforts, creaking harshly on the rusty hinges.

All was dark within, and Matilda having taken her lamp from the niche where she had placed it, passed over the threshold, and found herself in a chamber.

Here, however, nothing of moment, save some antique furniture, met her eyes; a door at the further extremity of the room was open; and passing through the space, found that she was at the head of a flight of stairs, which she imagined must be those which communicated with the several rooms of the turrets; and on ascending them, found she was right in her conjecture.

At the bottom of the stairs was a door which opened into

the great hall; and Matilda passing through it, entered the chapel, where with delight at having thus found an opportunity of paying her devotions, she poured forth a grateful prayer to heaven.

Matilda now used nightly, by this circuitous path, to visit the chapel, and devote her time in prayer to, and adoration of, Him from whom proceeded the calm repose her mind now enjoyed; for she now gradually withdrew her thoughts from the world, which she never more expected to visit, and fixed them on Him, before whose awful presence she knew, that one day, sooner or later, she must appear.

One night as she was engaged in fervent prayer at the altar, she thought she heard a noise in the vaults beneath: trembling with fear, she hastily placed her lamp behind a column, and endeavoured to shade its rays from observation.

A light arising from the passage that led from the subterraneous caverns into the chapel, now appeared, and, soon after, she saw the Abbot Bertrand enter the chapel, with a lamp, and pass through the grand aisle. Matilda, trembling for fear of being seen, stirred not till he had left the chapel, and then, with quick steps, retraced her way back to her chamber—she was afraid that he had been there, and, having discovered the way in which she had contrived to leave the place, was come in search of her, and perhaps, in his furious rage, might deprive her of her existence.

When she entered her apartment, however, she saw, with great satisfaction, that there was no appearance of his having visited it; and then replacing the pannel, she sat down to recover her breathless agitation. She now heard him above; and that night, to her great delight, he descended not into her chamber, but only let down the basket, in which were her provisions.

Matilda reflected on the great danger she ran of being discovered; and determined not to depart the place on that night in which she might expect him, through fear of being deprived of her only consolation.

The Abbot Bertrand had, at different times, related to her

all the circumstances which had taken place in the Castle, since the death of Sir Hugh De Seymour, and the marriage of De Fortebrand with her sister.

One night he informed her, that intelligence had been received that day from De Clifford, so long supposed dead; and that he was soon expected at the Castle.

This information, so unexpected, rendered Matilda for some time incapable of utterance—De Clifford alive! there was still then a tie for her on earth.—She concealed her emotions, as much as she was able, before the Abbot; but, when he retired, she threw herself on her knees, and thanked Heaven who had preserved him: but the idea that he might, in the certainty that she was no more, have paid those vows to another more happy object, which had so greatly interested her, struck to her heart. To know that he was married was more than she could have supported; but, however, as the Abbot had not made any mention of such a circumstance, she hoped and concluded he had not.

The Abbot now informed her of Sir Henry De Fortebrand's being found dead in the forest, and of his interment in the Castle vaults; which ceremony Matilda, from a distant passage, had witnessed; and, had remarked, as the torches, held by the domestics, threw their glare over the pale face of the Abbot, his great agitation, when he was reading the service of the dead over the coffin.

Some time now elapsed, and Matilda, according to custom, passed her nights in the chapel, excepting those on which the Abbot visited her with provisions.

One night he came to her much earlier than usual, and Matilda was pleased with the circumstance, because it prevented not her devotional exercises; and, taking up her lamp, she departed instantly, and arriving in the chapel, she proceeded directly to the altar: but what was her agitation on hearing the beloved voice of De Clifford calling on her, and seeing him kneeling before her tomb! trembling she concealed her small lamp, and listened to his miserable plaints, till at last, overcome with grief, his agitation forbade his further utterance.

Matilda could no longer keep silence, but, in a trembling voice, said—"De Clifford, be comforted;" and then, fearful of a discovery, retreated towards the hall.—She soon heard some quick steps behind her, and saw, by the beams of the moon, which streamed into the chapel, through the high window over the altar, De Clifford in pursuit of her. Hastily she quickened her steps; he however gained on her; when she, overcome with sensations of fear, at what must be her punishment, should the Abbot know of the circumstance, sunk, almost lifeless, on the marble pavement, and was, in the next moment, caught in the arms of De Clifford.

CHAPTER XX.

" 'Twas night, when nature was in sable drest,
    Tempestuous winds in hollow caves did rest;
    Impending rocks with slumber seem'd to bow,
    And drowsy mountains hung their heavy brow;
    The weary waves roll'd nodding on the deep,
    Or, stretch'd on oozy beds, they murmur'd in their sleep."

                                        BLACKMORE.

"Gracious heaven!" said De Clifford, "is this an illusion of the mind? or do I, indeed, again hold to my heart my adored Matilda?—Speak, fair angel—speak to me—resolve my doubts ere my senses forsake me!"

"It is indeed Matilda," said the agitated form, "but lost to thee for ever!"

"What word—what horrible sentence was that which passed thee? Lost to me for ever! but then another—tell me, Oh tell me quickly, ere my brain maddens."

"No," said the sighing maid, "another's I never shall be! But, alas! there is an oath, a dreadful oath, which I most incautiously have broken, and for which a certain death is my lot!"

"Good heaven! does not thy senses wander?" said De Clifford; "what meanest thou by a certain death? is not De Clifford
here to protect thee?—recall, my adored Matilda, thy scattered
thoughts!—tell me thy present situation, so long lost to the
world; and how thou, whom I saw claimed by the cold hand of
death, art again animated with the warm stream of life?"

Matilda had now, in some degree, recovered her agitation, and
gently disengaged herself from the agitated grasp of De Clifford.

"The story is long," replied the Lady Matilda; "but before I
can unfold to you my present situation, I must commune with
the reverend Father Oswald; for, alas! my present guilt weighs
heavy on my heart."

"Each word you speak, my adored Matilda, plunges me in a
maze of distracting doubts and apprehensions. What guilt? what
oath is it you allude to? Oh, my angelic love! tell me, tell your
own De Clifford."

"I may not," said Matilda, "until I have seen Father Oswald,
who only can direct me what to do. If, De Clifford, you will
promise to bring the holy Father with you, when night has again
drawn her sable curtain over the world, I will meet you here—till
then farewell."

So saying, she departed through the portal that opened into
the hall, and crossing it, entered the turrets.

De Clifford, lost in wonder and amazement at her speech, and
at her thus being again restored to the world, gazed on her form
until it was hid by the turret-portal; when, starting up, he hastily
left the chapel, and, proceeding with a hurried pace through the
vaults, left the Castle, and hastened to his own mansion.

De Clifford instantly proceeded to the chamber where Father
Oswald lay, and found the venerable monk in the silent embrace
of sleep.—Hastily he awoke him.

"Father," said he, "I have seen her, I have held her warm,
palpitating form in these arms!—She lives; Matilda yet lives!"

"The saints preserve your scattered senses!" exclaimed the
Father, hastily rising up. "What means my son, and why these

strange emotions, which betoken a disordered mind? I pray thee, quick, unfold thyself."

"Have I not told thee," said De Clifford, "that Matilda, my loved, my adored Matilda is alive—and wonderest thou then, Father, at my raptures?"

"Heaven restore thee!" said the alarmed Father; "thy Matilda is now a saint, in the bright realms above." So saying, he rose from off his couch, and was proceeding to summon the domestics, for he thought that the brain of De Clifford was unsettled.

De Clifford, guessing his intentions, hastily caught him by the arm: "Father," said he, "attend while I unfold my tale, which only thou must hear."

Father Oswald then desired he would compose himself, and he would not call the servants; and De Clifford, still holding the arm of the Father, with an agitated grasp, seated himself on the side of the couch, and then related to him the circumstance, of his having, that night, visited the tomb of Matilda, and of his having seen her there, and of her request that she might see Father Oswald the next night.

Oswald listened to the mysterious detail with astonishment. "The ways of heaven," said he, "are dark and intricate: but art thou sure, my son, that thy senses have not been deceived by some dream, which, painting what thou hast related to thy imagination, hath so won on thy senses, as to make thee believe it reality?"

"See Father," said De Clifford, "here is the key of the vaults: what further proof would you have than that, and my assertions, that what I have related to you is truth?"

"Enough, my son," returned Oswald; "I do believe thee— forasmuch as I do know of thee, I do conceive thee incapable of a falsehood. I will attend thee at the appointed time, the saints willing; but now, I pray thee, take repose, and rest thy harrassed senses."

"Repose, Father!" said De Clifford; "think you these eyes will close in slumber before I again see my adored Matilda, and know my doom?—Oh, no!"

"Then, my son, I will commune with thee; for this strange adventure hath stayed the soft influence of sleep from my eyes.— But see, the rising sun begins to illuminate the vaulted arch of heaven, and the ruddy east proclaims the swift-coming morn: return, my son, while I array myself, and offer up my orisons to the all-wise Disposer of events; who, in compassion to thy woes, hath made thee happy with the sight of her thou dost so fondly love, and entreat his blessing on our actions."

"And may thy pious prayer succeed, holy Father!" said De Clifford. "I will now leave you, and shall pace the hall till thou joinest me."

This said, he departed; and, from the lofty windows of the hall, watched the sun, as, with encreasing refulgence, it gilded the summits of the surrounding mountains.

Father Oswald now descended, and proceeded with De Clifford through the Castle gate, to walk in the extensive park, and converse on the occurrences of the past night, and which left not a vacuum in the mind of De Clifford.

Having arranged their departure, that evening, for the chapel of Berry Pomeroy Castle, they returned to the Castle; and impatiently did De Clifford watch the sun, and complained of his long sojourn on the face of nature.

At length the lengthening shadows shewed his decline, and soon after he sunk into the restless bosom of the ocean: and now the twilight had clad all things in her grey livery; the tuneful race had retired to seek repose, and in dreams repeated the blithe song of the day; the vapours of night arose from the earth, and the thickened gloom descended from the heavens; the song of the shepherd ceased; and now all was hushed in silence, save the watchful dog, that guarded the fleecy tribe; or the melancholy owl, that, from some ivy-mantled tower, broke on the silence around, with her harsh, discordant notes.

Father Oswald, with De Clifford, now passed through the massy gates of his Castle, and proceeded on their way to Berry Pomeroy.

As they had much time before them, ere it would be safe to approach that building, or enter the chapel, without danger of discovery, they slowly winded along the varied ground, sometimes rising on a gentle eminence, or gliding through the luxuriant vales; and at length they came to that over which the Castle of Berry Pomeroy proudly reared its head.

As some lights in the different casements shewed that the inhabitants had not yet retired for the night, they deemed it yet too early for their purpose; and, seating themselves on the trunk of a fallen tree, awaited till the lights should disappear.

At length, one after another was extinguished, and Father Oswald and De Clifford arose from the seat, and ascended the circuitous path that led from the valley up to the Castle.

Having opened a small door that led to the vaults, De Clifford struck a light, and, having illumined the lamp, proceeded through the silent passages with caution; for he was fearful lest he should again meet the mysterious visitant, who had so much aroused his curiosity the night before.

Having listened for some time, and no sound breaking on their attentive ears, they advanced to the steps which led to the chapel; and, ascending them, repaired to the altar, before which, having bowed with reverence, and besought heaven to prosper their designs, they waited, in breathless expectancy, the coming of the Lady Matilda.

As De Clifford had noticed that she had crossed the hall, when she left him, he slowly paced down the grand aisle, with the Father, and opened the lofty portals: here they waited some time; when at length a distant sound of footsteps was heard—and, an opposite door opening, discovered the Lady Matilda advancing towards the chapel.

De Clifford quickly flew forwards to meet her, and seizing her trembling hand, imprinted an ardent kiss on it.

"Fair angel," said he, "agreeable to your wishes, I have brought the venerable Father Oswald, who is now awaiting you at the portal of the chapel, happy beyond expression, that you, by some unknown, some mysterious circumstance, yet bless the earth and your De Clifford by your presence."

"De Clifford," said the Lady Matilda, "ere I can hold that converse with you which my heart wishes, I must first commune with the holy Father; conduct me to him."

Father Oswald now advanced, with visible agitation, and gave her his benediction, which she piously knelt to receive.

"Rise, fair daughter," said he; "I attend thee, full of wonder at thy appearance in this world, whom we so long mourned as dead: speak, fair daughter; unfold thy wishes to me."

"Father," said the Lady Matilda, "I have many words for your private ear: retire," said she, to De Clifford, "while at yon holy altar, I commune with Father Oswald; that done, I will, if so permitted, have further converse with thee."

De Clifford, sighing at her mysterious words, retired, and seated himself on a bench in the hall; and Matilda, walking by the side of Father Oswald, seemingly involved in some melancholy ruminations, entered the portals of the chapel, which she closed after her.

CHAPTER XXI.

"Let wretches, loaded hard with guilt, as I am,
    Bow with the weight, and groan beneath the burden;
    Creep, with the remnant of the strength they've left,
    Before the footstool of the heaven they've injur'd."

                                                    OTWAY.

"Heaven has but
Our sorrow for our sins; and then delights
To pardon erring man.—Sweet mercy seems
Its darling attribute, which limits justice."

                                                    DRYDEN.

THE Lady Matilda now advanced to the altar, and casting an impressive look on Father Oswald, said—

"Holy Father, I conjure thee, by Him who died for us, to

answer my questions, and to give me your holy advice, in what way I am to act. I stand convicted, Father," continued she, "in my own mind, of having broken an oath—a solemn promise that I made, and which I called the Deity to witness."

Father Oswald started, but spoke not.

Matilda then related to him every circumstance that had occurred from the time she revived, and found herself in the secret chamber; her having endeavoured, instigated by pity, on a former occasion, to speak words of comfort to De Clifford, when he was at her tomb bewailing her supposed loss; and also, actuated by the same motive, having done the same on the preceding night. "I call heaven to witness, Father," said she, "that I had no intention to break the oath I made to the Abbot, but so it has happened; and most severely do I blame myself for my heedless observance of it."

"Comfort thyself, my daughter," said Father Oswald; and his countenance, that had, at the different parts of her discourse, been clouded with grief, pity, and horror, now brightened up: "take comfort, my fair daughter; thou wouldest have been guiltless of sin, even if thou hadst intentionally broke an oath, administered to thee by the forceful act of setting instant death before thy affrighted eyes, to conceal the basest plot that ever entered the mind of man to conceive: but of all sin, in this instance, I do absolve thee—as does that Almighty Power, who, doubtless, brought about this discovery of so heinous, so black a crime: return we now, my fair daughter, to De Clifford, who, doubtless, awaits, with much impatience, our appearance."

This said, he conducted the Lady Matilda, who, comforted by the consoling discourse of Father Oswald, and now convinced in her own mind of her innocence, walked with a light heart to the portals of the chapel, which having opened, she saw De Clifford pacing, with agitated steps, the hall.

He instantly advanced towards her; and Father Oswald said,—"Behold, my son, thy affianced wife."

The countenance of the lovely Matilda was suffused with

blushes; whilst the enamoured De Clifford, falling on his knees before her, said—

"And will my Matilda suffer me to hope, that the ages of heart-felt grief I have experienced will be at last forgot in the blissful possession of her I so much adore?"

"My mind is still the same, De Clifford," said the confused Matilda.

"Blessings on thy sweet lips, for these kind words!" said the enraptured De Clifford; and taking her fair hand, imprinted a thousand kisses on it. "Will not my adored Matilda now," said he, "unfold the mysterious circumstances, which have again brought her to my happy sight?"

"Father Oswald," said Matilda, "now knows the whole, and he will make thee acquainted with my melancholy tale. The night is now far gone; even now methinks the eastern clouds are beginning to be tinged with the roseate hue of the morn: I must away, De Clifford, or the early-riser may discover me."

"Nay, my adored Matilda," said De Clifford, "surely you return no more to your dreary apartment?—Father, do you employ your eloquence."

"My fair daughter," said Oswald, "will, I trust, be guided by my advice, and proceed with me to the Monastery of Saint Austin's sisterhood, the venerable Abbess of which is my sister. Consider, my daughter," continued he, "your further stay is dangerous in this place; nor can I think you will wish to act contrary to my advice, and the wishes of De Clifford, who, I am convinced, would not leave you here to be exposed to further calamity."

"I yield, Father," said the Lady Matilda; "the saints guide and direct me."

The delighted De Clifford now proposed that they should instantly depart, as the morning was beginning to break; to which Matilda and Father Oswald immediately assented. They descended into the vaults, and soon were out of their gloomy recesses, and far from the lofty turrets of Berry Pomeroy.

The morning arising, in all its resplendent beauties, found

the happy travellers near where the sisterhood of St. Austin dwelt. Father Oswald, after waiting till such time as the venerable Abbess should arise, was at length admitted to her; and to her private ear disclosed the situation of the Lady Matilda, requesting that she might be admitted into the holy walls, until her enemies could no longer have it in their power to wreak their diabolical vengeance on her.

Gladly the Abbess consented, and Matilda being admitted, embraced her with much affection; and Father Oswald, pleased with the success that had attended his plans, retired, having promised to see the Lady Matilda daily, to bring her information of their proceedings.

He then rejoined the impatient De Clifford, and they consulted together on the best means to secure the Lady Elinor De Fortebrand, and her dark accomplice the Abbot Bertrand; knowing, that whilst they were at large, the existence of the Lady Matilda was in danger.

The result of their deliberation was, that De Clifford should commit the whole of the circumstances, which Father Oswald related to him, to paper, and then send it to the King, and await his decree.

This was accordingly done, and a horseman was instantly dispatched to the court. The recital of the Lady Matilda's wrongs so enraged the King, that he ordered both the Lady Elinor and the Abbot Bertrand to be seized to answer for the same.

This, as the reader will recollect, was, as far as related to the Lady Elinor, carried into effect; but the Pope's legate being informed of the order to take the Abbot into custody, would not allow such power to laical jurisdiction; and in conformity to a packet, which was sent by the Lady Matilda to him, he, in consequence, ordered that Father Oswald should take on him the high situation of Abbot; that Bertrand should be confined in the dungeons of the Abbey; and to be tried for his offence by the ecclesiastical court. These orders were implicitly obeyed, as has been hereinbefore shewn.

Meanwhile the circumstance of the Lady Matilda's having been discovered to be still in existence, was communicated to the delighted domestics of Berry Pomeroy Castle, every one was both surprised and pleased at so wonderful an intervention of Providence; and a day was fixed on which she should again enter those lofty towers; and preparations were made by the numerous retainers and vassals, to shew their joy, at having, once more, their beloved Lady to preside over them.

When the Lady Matilda, riding on her palfrey, attended by De Clifford, the Abbot Oswald, and a train of horsemen, came in sight of the Castle, the peasantry, attired in their best habiliments, ranged themselves on each side of the road, and, as she passed, respectfully bowed their heads, which salute she gracefully returned them; when she had passed, they threw their caps up, and rent the air with acclamations of joy.

The castellain of the Castle now approached, bearing in his hand the keys of the Castle gates, which he presented to the Lady Matilda, who, smiling, bade him still retain them in his trusty keeping for her.

The old man bowed, and seemed highly pleased with the compliment; and then preceded her over the drawbridge into the hall, through rows of the domestics, whose countenances shewed how delighted they were with the return of their beloved Lady.

Matilda spoke to them with her accustomed affability, and, directing the purveyor to make ready plentiful cheer for the vassals in the Castle hall, she retired to her apartments, accompanied by De Clifford and the Abbot.

Amidst the general joy at the Lady Matilda's return, her countenance was the only one which was clouded by grief. De Clifford observed it, and now that he had an opportunity, begged to know why it was so?

"Tell me," said he, "my adored Matilda, why those beauteous eyes bear the heavy weight of grief on their lids? and why a cloud of sorrow overhangs that intelligent countenance; now, too, when every heart around you swims in an ocean of happiness

and delight, at again beholding you reinstated in your possessions, free from the machinations of your enemies? Why partake
you not, my angelic love, in the general joy; and why do those
sighs betray the inward grief of your heart?"

"How, De Clifford," said the Lady Matilda, "is it possible
that I can be at ease, whilst my sister is enduring the pangs of
confinement? Oh, De Clifford! why did you so? was there no
other way?"

"Your own safety, my adored Matilda, demanded such a step;
but it was not at my instance she was so treated, but by the
positive order of the King. Your life would not be safe were she
at liberty; therefore, lament not, I pray you, the great necessity
there is for the harsh steps that have been made use of."

"I must ever lament them," said the Lady Matilda; "for, is she
not my sister, although she comported herself unlike one to me,
and occasioned me so many days and hours of misery? yet do I
freely forgive her all; and, even now, would hold her to my heart
with delight!"

"Heaven forbid," said Oswald, "that, unless her disposition is
no longer of such revengeful bearing, she ever again reside under
the same roof with thee, my daughter!"

Thus did the Abbot and De Clifford endeavour to disperse
the melancholy gloom that hung over the Lady Matilda; nor
would she listen to the voice of love from the lips of De Clifford,
until her sister's fate was known; and, with bitter sensations of
regret and horror, did she await the appointed day of trial, when,
by order of the King, she was to appear against the misguided
Lady Elinor De Fortebrand.

CHAPTER XXII.

"Misfortunes on misfortunes press upon me,
Swell o'er my head, like waves, and dash me down;
Despair, remorse, and shame, have torn my soul;
They hang, like winter, on my hopes,
And blast the golden promise of my year."

ROWE.

"He at the news,
Heart-struck, with chilling gripe of sorrow stood,
That all his senses bound."

MILTON.

MEANWHILE the Lady Elinor was kept in close confinement; nor was she suffered to have communication with any one; the man who attended her with provisions being the only person who entered her apartment.

For some time after she had been taken there, she was so confounded at the event, that the faculties of speech were denied her; and she reclined on a couch in the room, for many hours, almost in a state of insensibility.

At length, the strong workings of her rage and despair in some degree subsided; and she then began to reflect by whose means, or for what reason she had been apprehended.

The Abbot Bertrand was the only person at whom the eye of her suspicions glanced; but it was not likely that he would divulge transactions which would criminate himself; still, as there was no one else, who could have done it? she could but suspect him; for she well knew no suspicion was entertained of the way by which the existence of Matilda was terminated; and though the arrow, found in the body of Sir Ethelred De Fortebrand, was known to have belonged to the Castle armoury, yet the remembrance of the circumstance had begun to subside;

nor was there any clue which would guide the hand of justice on her, for her participation in that nefarious act, except through the means of the Abbot.

Thus, bewildered in a maze of doubts and conjectures, passed the solitary hours of the Lady Elinor.

From the casement of the chamber of the small Castle she was confined in, and which stood on a commanding elevation, the scene that appeared was rich with all the varied beauties of nature. Beneath her glided the Dart, whose pebbly bottom could clearly be discovered through the transparent waves.

To the right was seen the bold shores that confined its devious course, whose romantic sides were covered with hanging woods, that dipped their leafy inhabitants into the clear waves.

On the left the river, dividing into several small streams, extended over the level surface of the country, and aided the efforts of the toiling peasantry. From the window too she could see part of the grounds of De Clifford Castle; this prospect, whenever it met her view, struck with agony to her heart, and hastily, with tearful eyes, would she avert her painful gaze. De Clifford, to whom she had hoped to be united, was now lost to her for ever—herself confined for some crime of which she was ignorant; and fearful that it might be the one which dwelt now heavily on her mind—namely, the murder of her sister; for the care with which she was guarded, and the numerous forces that had been sent to take her, proved her offence to be no trifling one.

The warden of the Castle, one morning, entered her chamber —"Lady," said he, "I am ordered to notify to you the near approach of the day on which you are to be tried."

"To be tried!" said the Lady Elinor, faintly, and greatly agitated; "know you for what?—explain, I pray you, the impeachment which rests on me."

"That I may not, Lady," replied the warden, "without diso-bedience of my orders. If thou art guilty, Lady, what avails the relation? thou knowest it already; if innocent, it little imports thee, for thy just dealing will soon appear. Soon as the morrow's sun hath traversed one quarter of his diurnal course, I shall wait on thee, Lady, to conduct you to the hall of this Castle, where the King wills you should be arraigned."

"'Tis well," replied, indignantly, the Lady Elinor, whose anger was raised by the import of certain parts of his speech. "Thou knowest well, warden, I shall be here, therefore it was of little consequence that thou hast thus disturbed me with thy information; the morrow would have been equally fitting."

"I but obeyed my orders, Lady; Sir Henry De Clifford would have it so."

"Sir Henry De Clifford!" said the Lady Elinor; "and is it he at whose order I am confined?"

"I thought, Lady, thou knewest that," replied the warden; "it is no secret."

"Leave me, warden, I wish to be alone;" so saying she covered her pale face in her garments, and her convulsed body shewed how much that unexpected information had affected her.

The warden, making his obeisance, retired, and left the miserable Elinor to her torturing meditations.

Here, then, was the secret explained: the Abbot had been faithless—the murder of her sister was discovered, and De Clifford had been the means of having her brought to justice; and all she could now expect was to meet the due reward of her crimes, from the hands of the executioner.

"Rather," said she, "shall these hands terminate my existence!—rather would I dash myself against these walls, than suffer myself to be made a public spectacle of scorn and contempt."

In these ruminations did she pass the night; sleep came not to her agitated eyes, and the morning sun found her pacing her chamber with restless inquietude.

Soon the portal of her room was thrown open, and the warden entered.

"Lady," said she, "the court is now awaiting thy presence— permit me to conduct thee to it."

The Lady Elinor, without reply, trembling with agitation,

followed him through the corridor, and down the long flight of steps; at the foot of which was a door that opened into the hall, into which he conducted her; and pointing to a seat which was placed apart from the rest, took his station near her.

Elinor, casting her eyes round, saw that the judges, who had been deputed by the King to try her, were assembled.

A band of soldiers, with their bright pikes, were stationed round the court; and on the opposite side, with evident emotion, Lady Elinor saw De Clifford, whose countenance seemed full of joy and content. The sight was more than she could support, and, with a heartfelt sigh, she turned away her head.

The herald commanding silence, and having demanded if Lady Elinor De Fortebrand was in the court, and received her answer, then said—

"Is there any one in this court who hath aught to alledge against the Lady Elinor De Fortebrand? if so, let him appear, before the third blast of the trumpet render his allegations fruitless."

He then motioned to the trumpeter, who instantly filled the echoing hall with his loud notes.—A pause then ensued—and De Clifford said, "Behold the man, most noble Lords, who rises up to accuse the Lady Elinor."

"And who art thou?" demanded the herald.

"I am called Sir Henry De Clifford," returned he.

"Proceed then, Sir Henry De Clifford, and state to the court thy knowledge of the Lady Elinor's transactions for which she is thus publicly cited to appear."

"I do accuse the Lady Elinor of the guilty act of devising, with Father Bertrand, lately Abbot of Ford, on the means of depriving her innocent sister, the Lady Matilda De Pomeroy, of life; and that, in consequence of such consultation, the Father Bertrand presented her with a certain mixture, which he affirmed would effect the purpose; and which the Lady Elinor, with that most foul intent, presented to her unsuspecting sister, who most unhappily drank it."

Here De Clifford paused; and the herald demanded of the Lady Elinor, if she were guilty of the crime alledged against her by Sir Henry De Clifford?

"I do deny the charge," said the Lady Elinor, faintly: "where are your proofs? It is well known by all who saw her, that the dart of death, which stopped the vital current of the Lady Matilda's life, was not impelled by the hand of poison; and I defy the accuser even to prove that such a potion as he mentioned was administered."

"For that purpose, my Lords," said De Clifford, "another witness must be produced: allow me to trespass on your patience a few moments, while I haste to bring an evidence of my assertions."

This said, he left the court, which was buried in profound silence; every one anxiously looking towards the door at which he had departed, in expectation of his re-appearance.

He re-entered in a few minutes with Father Oswald, supporting in their arms a Lady, who seemed almost unable to move.

As soon as Elinor saw her, she shrieked aloud with horror:— "O God!" she exclaimed, "the spirit of the departed Matilda is come to accuse me, her murderess! Oh! 'tis too much!" Here, with a deep groan, she fell lifeless on the floor.

Matilda, owing to the agitation she herself was in, at thus being obliged to come forward to criminate her sister, was unable to render her any assistance; and sat trembling on a seat prepared for her, while Father Oswald and De Clifford advanced to raise her up.

The court, who knew not what to think of the mysterious veil which appeared to envelope the case in question, remained in their several stations, anxiously awaiting when the returning senses of the Lady Elinor would permit the trial to proceed.

At length she recovered, and the people who had been busied in restoring her to animation retired—she again fixed her eyes on the agitated form of Matilda.

"Who, and what art thou," said she, "that thus appears in the likeness of her who is no more?—who, alas, these aching eyes saw claimed by the cold hand of death? speak to me, I conjure you."

"Hapless Elinor!" said Matilda, "behold thy own sister, saved from that death thou didst design for me, by the Abbot Bertrand, who deceived thee, with regard to the qualities of the mixture he gave thee, and which, alas, thou ministered with an intent to destroy her who loved thee with the sincerest affection!"

"The saints be praised!" said the pallid Elinor, "that the dreadful crime dwells not with me: alas, I do confess me of my foul intents, and here, a penitent, await my too just sentence."

The Lady Elinor having thus declared her guilt, the judge then addressed her.

"After the words which have passed the lips of the Lady Elinor De Fortebrand, it becomes my duty to pass on thee the sentence of the injured laws of thy country, which do expressly order, that they who are found guilty of designing the death of another, even though the nefarious crime may not have been committed, yet are, in effect, equally culpable, and are therefore condemned to die. I do, therefore, by virtue of them, sentence the Lady Elinor—"

"Stop—O, stay your words one moment!" cried the frantic Matilda, throwing herself at the feet of the judge; "behold her sister, her intended victim pleads for her: I conjure thee, by the blessed Virgin, doom her not to death!—O, judge, be merciful! Here will I stay, prostrate before thee, till thou hear, and accedest to my request."

"Rise, Lady," said the judge; "the laws of thy country must not be disobeyed; and," continued he, in a solemn voice, "I do therefore sentence the Lady Elinor to die; but thy request I will make known to the King, who may, moved with mercy and compassion, revoke the sentence, which my duty obliges me to utter."

This said, the judge arose and dismissed the court; the Lady

Elinor was conducted to her chamber, and the miserable Matilda, attended by De Clifford and Father Oswald, returned to Berry Pomeroy Castle.

CHAPTER XXIII.

"A kind of weight hangs heavy at my heart;
My flagging soul flies under her own pitch,
Like fowl in air too damp, and lags along,
As if she were a body in a body,
And not a mounting substance made of fire:
My senses too are dull and stupified;
Their edge rebated: Sure some ill approaches,
And some fatal spirit knocks upon my breast,
To tell my fate's at hand."

DRYDEN.

THUS was Father Bertrand conducted to the dungeons of the Abbey, of which he was so late the proud superior; but now, divested of that situation he had waded through blood and deep hypocrisy to possess, was become the wretched inmate of its dreary prison, without hopes of escape.

His suspicions immediately fell on Elinor, whom he thought was the only person who could have betrayed him; but, on a mature reflection, that seemed so highly improbable, that he banished the idea.

Of Matilda he could not entertain any fears; and, by this time, she must have perished for want, in her solitary apartment. The only thing that seemed most probable to him was, that he had been discovered, by some person, to be that Walter who had murdered Sir Edgar Fitz-Auburne; and that, at last, justice, though tardy in her movements towards him, at length held over his guilty head her retributive sword.

The day of his trial being arrived, he was conducted to the hall of the Abbey, where were convened the whole community, with Father Oswald, then Abbot, at their head.

Bertrand, casting his eyes around, saw De Clifford, who also attended there to accuse him.

The Abbot, who had been charged with full power from the Pope's legate, to examine into the nature of the offence of Father Bertrand, now received from De Clifford the charge against him, which amounted to the having, by undue means, and unbecoming the holy order he belonged to, detained in a long captivity the Lady Matilda De Pomeroy.

Bertrand listened with astonishment to the charge—astonishment, because he could not conceive how it had so happened that Matilda had been discovered; for he well knew that he had rendered it impossible for her to escape, by his having secured the door of the upper chamber; and then again the oath she had taken, even supposing she could have got out of her prison, would, he thought, be an effectual bar to her divulging her situation.

He was, however, most pleased to find that this was the only charge against him, since the punishment could not extend to his life, which, had he been discovered to be Walter, must have inevitably been the case, as the proofs against him there were too strong to admit of hopes of escape. He, therefore, immediately, with affected contrition, owned the deed.

The Abbot, having then committed the minutes of their proceedings to paper, dispatched a messenger with them to the Pope's legate, to know his further pleasure; and Father Bertrand was re-conducted to his cell.

The officer who commanded the armed soldiery that were sent to apprehend the Lady Elinor and the Abbot, had not yet received his order to depart, and therefore still remained with his men encamped, on the meadow fronting the Abbey.

The same morning that Father Bertrand had been tried, one of the soldiers, who had been in the hall during that time, came to his tent, and begged to speak a few words with him.

He then informed him that he had strong suspicions that Father Bertrand, whom that day he had seen in the hall, was no other than one Walter, who had been discovered to be the perpetrator of a most dreadful murder, but who had hitherto escaped the searching eye of justice.

The officer, astonished at the circumstance, demanded of the man his name; which he informed him was Hubert.

He then related to him the circumstances relative to the murder; and of his having, actuated by the promises of Walter, accused Sir Alfred Fitz-Auburne, as having slain his father, Sir Edgar, with the sword of Sir Hugh Trevanion, which he, Hubert, had procured for him; and that it had appeared on the trial, that he, Sir Alfred, was only the instigator, but that it was Walter who had perpetrated the dreadful deed. Hubert added, that he was not quite certain as to the person of Father Bertrand being that of Walter, but, if he could see him again, he would assure himself of that circumstance.

The officer, having listened to Hubert's relation with much attention, now judged it expedient to acquaint the Abbot, Father Oswald, with the circumstance.

He therefore dismissed the man, telling him that he would inform the Abbot with what he had related to him; and that if he deemed it fit, he should again have an opportunity of seeing Father Bertrand.

He then immediately proceeded to the Abbot Oswald, and informed him of the surmise of the soldier; and then requested to know his wishes respecting it.

Father Oswald having considered the detail of the officer, thought it would be advisable to let Hubert again see Bertrand, that he might be convinced whether he had not been mistaken as to the person; he therefore directed, that, to prevent suspicion, he should attend in the habit of a lay brother, the following morning, and be admitted into the cell of the Monk, under pretence of bringing him his daily food, when he might convince himself if his suspicions were just.

Accordingly, the next morning the soldier was habited as the Abbot had directed, and appeared before Bertrand with his food.

The Monk, who was absorbed in a deep reverie, scarcely observed him; and Hubert had full opportunity of bringing his features to his recollection; and, when he left the cell, declared, that he had no manner of doubt, as to the identity of his person.

The Abbot, therefore, having collected the details of the peasant, of the acts of Walter, then known as the Father Bertrand, sent another messenger to the Pope's legate, with the packet, informing him of these further discoveries.

When the Legate received information of these extraordinary events, he determined himself to attend the trial that Bertrand must undergo, in consequence of the peasant Hubert's accusation; and having explained the circumstance to the King, it was agreed, that although Bertrand was now a member of the church, yet as the crimes he was accused of were committed before he had entered into that holy society, that an equal number of the laity should attend his trial, with the holy fathers; and that the Abbot Oswald should preside over the whole.

This being arranged, the Legate set out, attended by six of the laity, who were deputed to assist on this occasion, with such witnesses to identify his person, from the Castle of Fitz-Auburne, as were necessary; for his guilt had been fully proved before, and therefore nothing now remained but to prove that he was that Walter who had been the dark agent of Sir Alfred Fitz-Auburne, who had, on the fatal scaffold, publicly atoned for his dark offences.

As soon as the Legate arrived at the Abbey of Ford, he directed preparations to be instantly made for the trial; and, on the following morning, Father Bertrand was summoned from his cell to attend the court.

When he arrived in the hall, he was at a loss to account for the mysterious and solemn appearance of every thing. At the further end, on a lofty throne, sat Father Oswald, the Abbot, as judge; and on each side below him, sat twelve men, one half of whom were friars, and the other half were laity.

As a spectator, richly adorned in his superb habiliments,

appeared the Pope's legate, with his numerous attendants; in the hall the remainder of the Fathers sat in different parts; and behind were ranged a line of soldiery.

A profound silence was observed; and Father Oswald, addressing himself to Bertrand, demanded if, formerly, he had not borne the name of Walter; and whether he had not been a domestic in the Castle of Fitz-Auburne?

This question, so little expected, so little looked for, made the limbs of Bertrand shake with convulsive agitations: for a long while, unable to give utterance to his words, he was silent; but at length, on the question being again repeated, he faintly articulated—"No."

"Weigh well, Father Bertrand, what thou sayest," said the Abbot Oswald; "know, that there is One above, from whose searching eyes no secrets are hid; speak then, wilt thou solemnly deny that thou art not the person I have represented to thee?"

"I will," replied Bertrand.

"Stop thy words, give not utterance to an untruth," mildly returned the Father Oswald; "for we have full evidence that thou art the person alluded to."

He then beckoned to Hubert to advance from the rest of his companions, who, having immediately obeyed the summons, stood before the horror-struck eyes of Bertrand, who now gave himself up as lost.

Hubert being demanded if he could solemnly swear that the person he saw before him had formerly been known by the name of Walter, and that he was the person who had been known, by the confession of Sir Alfred, to have committed the murder of Sir Edgar Fitz-Auburne, instantly affirmed the same; and the other domestics, who had been with him in Fitz-Auburne Castle, having seen him, agreed in their firm assurance of his being Walter.

No doubts being now entertained, the Abbot thus addressed the Father, and the laical deputation.

"Have you, holy Father, and you, my sons, any doubts among

you of this person who now stands before you, being other than that Walter, who is well known to have committed the crime wherewith he is charged? if ye have, speak, and let us not act rashly; for it best becomes us to be merciful to each other, who all stand in so much need of mercy: speak then your doubts, if ye have any."

"We have none, holy Father," returned the monks and the deputation.

"Then, Walter," said the Abbot, "or, as thou art best known amongst us, Bertrand, thou standest condemned of the horrible crime of murder, for which dreadful offence thy forfeit life can only be offered up as an expiation; and Heaven grant it may be so considered, when thou appearest before the throne of the Almighty Ruler of the World. The time and manner of thy death his Holiness's Legate, who is here present before you, will, in his wisdom, appoint: prepare thy guilty soul, meanwhile, my Brother, for the awful event, and think of an hereafter."

This said, he bowed low to the Legate, and dismissed the court; and the miserable Bertrand, unable to stand, through the violence of his agitation, was borne to his cell.

CHAPTER XXIV.

"But mercy
Is an attribute to God himself;
And earthly power doth then show likest God's,
When mercy seasons justice."

SHAKESPEARE.

"Heaven, to whose all-piercing eyes
Lie open the most obscure recesses of the heart,
Is not to be deceiv'd by specious shews;
And ne'er forgets the murderer in his wrath."

HAYWARD.

THE King having received the detail of the trial of the Lady

Elinor De Fortebrand from the judge, commended the proceedings; yet, being pleased with the affection shewn to her by her much-wronged sister, he remitted the sentence of death, and ordered her to be confined in some convent, whose strict rules and rigid penances would reclaim her from her evil ways, and be of the utmost good to the welfare of her soul; and accordingly fixed on the Convent of Saint Anna, which was situate at Buckfastleigh, and near to the Abbey of that name.

Agreeable to his instructions, the warden waited on the Lady Elinor, to inform her of this movement in her favour. She received the intelligence with much agitation, for death would have been far more preferable to her haughty spirit, than being condemned to wear out her existence in the dull monotonous life of a nun.

"And when, warden," said she, "is this hateful sentence to be carried into execution?"

"This night, Lady, a car will attend thee, to convey thee to the convent appointed by the King, and which is distant but a few leagues."

When the dark-robed evening approached, the warden again entered the Lady Elinor's chamber.

"Lady," said he, "the attendants await thee at the outward gate—suffer me to conduct thee to them."

The Lady Elinor now arose, and descending into the courtyard, saw the car, into which she stepped, and was conveyed, under the care of a party of horsemen, to the Convent of Saint Anna, where she was compelled, the next morning, to take the vow of seclusion; the Pope's Legate, who had been consulted on the occasion, having agreed to dispense with the preparatory year.

His Holiness's Legate approved of the sentence that the Abbot Oswald had awarded against Bertrand; but, as he had formerly bore the high office of Superior, he was unwilling that the execution of the sentence should be public, or that his blood should be shed.

He therefore ordered that three days be given to Bertrand, to prepare himself, and that on the evening of the fourth, he be buried alive—a punishment dreadful in the extreme, but common in those ages.

He then left the Abbey, and proceeded, with his train and the party of soldiers, to the place where the King then kept his court.

Meanwhile a Monk was dispatched to the cell of the wretched Bertrand, to inform him of the sentence; also to acquaint him that he would be obliged to attend every day to see the grave dug, in which he was to be laid.

Horror-struck at this dreadful intelligence, Bertrand fell on the stone floor of his cell, deprived of his senses, and for a long time lay motionless; at last, deep groans issued from his tortured breast.

"Oh, Father," said he, "recall thy words; hast thou not some instrument by thee, some means which in pity thou couldest give me, that I may, myself, hinder the execution of so horrible a doom? To be interred alive—to be buried in the cold womb of the earth, while the stream of life flows in my veins, and all the senses are awake—Oh 'tis horrible indeed!"

Maddened with his agonizing sensations, he dashed his head on the stones, but was prevented from putting a period to his existence, by some of the lay brothers who attended.

For a long time he struggled to get from their grasp; at length, weary with his exertions, he became unable to make further resistance, and was led, by order of the Abbot, to the spot which had been appointed for his grave, in unconsecrated ground.

The holy Fathers were then assembled, and Bertrand was obliged to view the lay brothers begin to dig up the earth, which was so shortly to cover him; for a while he shut up his eyes, but then the noise the mattocks made in opening the ground, smote like daggers to his breast.

At length the Abbot ordered the men to cease their work; and then solemnly reminded Bertrand that a third part of his grave was dug—and in a pious exhortation, besought him to prepare for death, by making atonement to offended Heaven, for the dark crimes he had committed.

Bertrand listened, but replied not; his feelings were too great, too dreadful to allow him the power of speech; and he was supported, almost lifeless, from the solemn scene to his cell, where two of the brethren were ordered to watch him, lest he should commit further violence on himself, and add to his other crimes that terrible one of self-destruction.

Bertrand passed the remainder of that day and night in horrible agonies of mind; his deep and dreadful lamentations were distinctly heard in the most retired parts of the Abbey: he refused all sustenance, and repeatedly besought the brothers to give him the means of present death, so to avoid the horrible one that awaited him.

The second morning now arrived; and Bertrand was again taken to the fatal spot, where he saw another portion of his grave dug, and was again exhorted by the Abbot Oswald to prepare.

Bertrand could only answer in deep-toned groans; and when the ceremony ended, he was again taken to his cell.

Still refusing all nourishment, he passed the second day in a similar manner to the last; but his strength beginning to abate, with the constant wearing of grief and despair, his lamentations were not so audible.

On the third morning, Bertrand, no longer able to walk, was borne to the grave. This day the men completed their task; and the fearful eyes of Bertrand glanced into the gloomy cavity, which he was soon to inhabit, and which, trembling through all his tortured frame, he contemplated.

"Behold thy grave," said the Abbot, "behold, oh Bertrand, the spot where thy mortal form is to be laid, where thou wilt render up thy guilty existence; take heed that thy few remaining hours are passed in prayers to the offended Deity; prostrate thyself before His altar, confess thy sins, and implore His mercy."

The wretched Bertrand, overcome with the emotions of his mind, and which his weak frame rendered him unable to support, sunk senseless on the cold earth, and, for a short time, was insensible to the horrors of his situation.

When he revived, he found himself in his cell, with Father Oswald by his side; he essayed to raise himself up, but was unable, his grief, and his having abstained from all food, had so much weakened his frame; his eyes were deep sunk in his head, his cheeks hollow, and his whole countenance exhibited approaching dissolution.

Father Oswald for a long time conversed with him; but Bertrand was unable to reply, except in hollow groans, to the demands of the Abbot, respecting his belief in the blessed saints.

"I conjure thee, my unhappy son," said the Father Oswald, "as thou hopest and lookest up for heaven's bliss, make me some sign of thy repentance of thy ill-spent life."

Bertrand now raised his languid eyes to heaven, and clasped his hands together.

The Abbot understood the sign, and praying the saints to take him into their blessed keeping, with deep melancholy impressed on his intelligent countenance, retired from the awful scene.

Bertrand continued in that inanimate state the whole of the night; and early the next morning some of the lay brethren entered the cell, bearing a bier.

Bertrand started at the sight, which seemed to recall him from the torpid insensibility he had so long lain in.

The brother now, agreeable to his instructions, took off the emaciated body of Bertrand the habiliments of the order, and clothed him in the vestments of the grave; that done, he was laid on the bier, and borne to the chapel.

Here were assembled all the Fathers of the Abbey; and as soon as Bertrand, who was unable to move, was laid before the altar, the monks chaunted a solemn dirge, and the funeral service was read.

Bertrand awoke, as if from a sleep, at the solemn voice of the Abbot, as he performed the rituals, and, exerting all his force, threw himself off the bier, and dashed himself on the steps of the altar, groaning with sensations the most horrible to be conceived; at last, stunned with the fall, he lay insensible, which circumstance delayed, for a short time, the performance of the service.

He was at length replaced on the bier; and when at last he opened his eyes, the Abbot concluded the ceremony.

Now the Abbot descended the steps of the altar, with a slow and solemn pace, striving in vain to conceal the grief that oppressed him.

When he had passed the bier, the ill-fated Bertrand was borne after him, by four of the lay brothers, after them followed the train of the fathers, with deep melancholy seated in their pale countenances; no sound was heard, except the low groans of Bertrand, and the deep sighs of the Fathers.

Thus they proceeded to the grave; and Bertrand, now almost senseless, was let down in it.

A solemn dirge was then sung, by the trembling voices of the fathers, and the remainder of the service for the dead performed.

When, agreeable to one part of the discourse, some earth was thrown upon him, Bertrand started, and raising his eyes to heaven, for the first time since his sentence was known to him, faintly said—

"Fathers, remember me in your prayers, and oh, may the blessed saints above take me, a repentant sinner, to their holy keeping!"

The rest of his speech was inarticulate; and soon he only moved his lips, without any sound proceeding from them.

The Abbot and the whole train threw themselves on their knees, and besought the mercy of heaven on his sinful soul; then, rising up, the Abbot gave the signal, and the earth was thrown into the grave.

A faint groan was heard, and, for a few moments, the earth was convulsed; the heap now increased on him, and soon the grave was closed up.

The venerable train now retired, oppressed with deep melancholy, to the Abbey; and withdrew to their cells, to reflect on the solemn scene they had just witnessed.

CHAPTER XXV.

"The breathing flute's soft notes are heard around,
And the shrill trumpets mix their silver sound;
The vaulted roofs with echoing music ring—
These touch the vocal stop, and these the tremb'ling string."

POPE.

—————————"They lov'd;
'Twas friendship, heighten'd by the mutual wish.
Th' enchanting hope, and sympathetic glow,
Beam'd from the mutual eye. Devoting all
To love, each was to each a dearer self,
Supremely happy in the awaken'd power
Of giving joy."
THOMSON.

THUS ended the life of the guilty Bertrand, affording an awful example to those who, impelled by ambition, or worse passions, step into the stream of guilt; for a while they behold the current glide harmless by them, and, confident of safety, proceed farther into the flood, which at length overwhelms them, at the moment they are least sensible of their danger, in the hidden whirlpools of destruction.

The Lady Elinor too, at last reaped the reward of her ill-spent life, in being secluded for her life, with the gloomy inhabitants of a cloister, which, to a disposition like her's, was perhaps a punishment more severe than death.

Had the part she took, in the taking off of Sir Ethelred De Fortebrand been discovered, the laws of her country must have been put in force, and she would have suffered an ignominious exit; but that all-seeing Providence, from whom no secrets of our hearts are hid, willed that that atrocious act should not be brought to light, that she might have time to repent of her crimes ere she was called to answer for them at the throne of judgement, where the sinful actions of our lives appear unveiled, unglossed by specious pretences, or outward shew, and cover the guilty mind with unutterable confusion—while our virtuous deeds, like the bright beams of the sun, which chase away the misty vapours of the night, animate us with hope and confidence, in the never-failing goodness of our blessed Judge, and enable us to support the awful hour.

The Lady Matilda being at length relieved from her anxiety, respecting the fate of her sister, the Lady Elinor De Fortebrand, De Clifford again ventured to speak to her on the subject of marriage.

"Receive," said the smiling Matilda, offering him her hand, "this pledge, that, as soon as the remembrance of the recent occurrences are in some degree effaced, I will no longer refuse you the full possession of it."

De Clifford, taking her hand, imprinted many grateful kisses on it, and retired to communicate her reply to his venerable friend, the Abbot Oswald, who participated in his happiness.

At length the day was fixed for the nuptials of Sir Henry De Clifford and the Lady Matilda De Pomeroy; and preparations were made to celebrate it with all possible splendor.

On that morning the halls of the Castle of Berry Pomeroy resounded to the blithesome notes of the minstrels, joy reigned in every breast, and smiles appeared on every countenance.

Soon a cheerful train approached the Castle, and the valleys re-echoed to the sound of martial music.

In the center of the cavalcade rode, on his well reined courser, De Clifford, having his banner, helmet, and shield, borne before him.

The Abbot Oswald rode on a palfrey by his side, and seemed, in the participation of the general joy, to have forgot his advanced years.

The gates of Berry Pomeroy Castle were thrown open at their approach; and as Sir Henry De Clifford entered the hall, the Lady Matilda advanced to meet him.

"Fair angel," said De Clifford, "behold the blissful moment is at length arrived, which will ensure me the possession of you, whom I must ever so tenderly adore. Father," said he to the Abbot, "we now wait your holy office."

This said, he conducted the blushing Matilda towards the chapel, preceded by the Abbot Oswald, who then bestowed on him that treasure which none but himself deserved.

De Clifford received the lovely recompence for all his afflictions, with a heart overflowing with joy and gratitude, to that Providence who had directed him to be the means of rescuing her from her solitary seclusion, and finally of raising the retributive arm of justice against her oppressors.

All was peace, joy and happiness at the Castle of Berry Pomeroy; contentment made it her chosen seat.

The venerable Abbot Oswald was long a witness to the mutual happiness of his amiable friends; and at length exchanged his earthly existence, which had been one scene of piety, for an eternal joyous life in the bright realms above.

The Lady Matilda and De Clifford sincerely regretted his loss; but the conviction that he was now supremely blessed, restrained the unavailing stream of grief.

Here the pen stops, satisfied with having endeavoured to pourtray, in lively colours, the evils resulting from an indulgence of our sinful passions; and the final happiness that ever will attend the upright mind.

The happy De Clifford and the lovely Lady Matilda exhibited a picture of conjugal felicity, which even the relentless hand of Time could not injure or sully; the colours were always bright, unclouded by the dark vapours of strife; and they beheld their offspring rising around them, with every principle of virtue, and rectitude of conduct, deep planted in their infant breasts.

Thus terminates our history—and should our readers have been able to extract our moral from these pages, the intent will have been most fully answered.—To paint vice in its true colours, to shew its deformity, and how finally its due punishment falls, with unerring weight, on the guilty head, and to shew the blessings that ever will attend on virtuous deeds, has been our aim—our wish has been to blend instruction with amusement: how far we have succeeded must be left to the world to judge—our intent was good.

THE END.

www.ingramcontent.com/pod-product-compliance
Lightning Source LLC
Chambersburg PA
CBHW011650010726
47496CB00012B/3017